THE BLACKSTONE SHE-WOLF

ALSO BY ALICIA MONTGOMERY

THE TRUE MATES SERIES

Fated Mates
Blood Moon
Romancing the Alpha
Witch's Mate
Taming the Beast
Tempted by the Wolf

THE LONE WOLF DEFENDERS SERIES

Killian's Secret
Loving Quinn
All for Connor

THE BLACKSTONE MOUNTAIN SERIES

The Blackstone Dragon Heir
The Blackstone Bad Dragon
The Blackstone Bear
The Blackstone Wolf
The Blackstone Lion

The Blackstone She-Wolf

The Blackstone She-Bear

ABOUT THE AUTHOR

Alicia Montgomery has always dreamed of becoming a romance novel writer. She started writing down her stories in now long-forgotten diaries and notebooks, never thinking that her dream would come true. After taking the well-worn path to a stable career, she is now plunging into the world of self-publishing.

facebook.com/aliciamontgomeryauthor
twitter.com/amontromance
bookbub.com/authors/alicia-montgomery

This is a work of fiction. Names, characters, businesses, places, events, locales, and incidents are either the products of the author's imagination or used in a fictitious manner. Any resemblance to actual persons, living or dead, or actual events is purely coincidental.

Copyright © 2018 Alicia Montgomery
Cover design by Melody Simmons
Edited by Red Ribbon Editing

All rights reserved.

THE BLACKSTONE SHE-WOLF
BLACKSTONE MOUNTAIN 6

ALICIA MONTGOMERY

PROLOGUE

"Motherfucking douche nozzle!" Kate Caldwell cursed as she slammed her palm on her keyboard. She reached over to her side table, grabbed the half-empty can of *POWERJOLTZ* energy drink, and took a healthy swig. Swinging back to face the computer monitor, she took a deep breath and pressed "unmute" on her phone.

"Are you there, Miss Caldwell?"

"I'm here, Mr. Dennis." *You twatwaffle.* She bit her lip so hard to stop herself from saying that out loud it nearly bled. "Now, tell me again what's wrong with the buttons for your app *this time?*"

"Well, I think you need to move them more to the left," Martin Dennis said.

"Uhm, you told me to move them to right the last time," she reminded him.

He ignored her. "And also, the background is too blue."

"But your last email said, and I quote, 'make the background blue-er.'"

"Yes, but now it's too blue."

Kate pressed the mute button again and let out a scream. After two seconds, she unmuted the call. "So, a little *less* blue but not *too* blue." This time, she couldn't stop the sarcastic tone in her voice.

Dennis let out an unhappy grunt. "Is there a problem, Miss Caldwell? You know, I could go to another designer who can do this for us."

"No, no problem at all." Her fingers turned into claws and scratched down the leather arm rests of her chair. *Damn wolf.* "I'll get to work."

"Great, great!" he said. "Now, before you go, there are a couple of other things I need to talk about …."

Kate gave a silent groan and glanced at the clock. She really needed to get out of here *now*. As if it wasn't bad enough, the notifications on her personal phone were blowing up as Martin Dennis kept droning on and on about another project they were working on.

She wanted to tear her hair out. But Barkely Industries was one of her best anchor clients, and she needed the money. Sure, if she had taken a full-time job at Lennox Corp. she'd be raking in the dough, but Kate preferred the freedom of being a freelance software engineer and app designer. There was nothing like being her own boss and dictating her own hours, but it was times like this when she dreamt of having a corner office, putting her heels up on her desk, and ordering her minions around.

"… did you get that last thing, Miss Caldwell?" he asked.

"What? Uh, of course Mr. Dennis." What the fuck had he been droning on about? "I really should get off the phone now, so I can make these changes for you."

"Right. I'll expect the changes by morning. Have a good day, Miss Caldwell."

Ugh, she hated how he always called her that. No matter how many times she told him to call her Kate, he insisted on calling her 'Miss Caldwell' in that condescending sneer of his. "You too." *Thundercunt.*

Kate had never been so happy to end a call. The line had barely dropped before she was on her feet, grabbing her phone, jacket, and keys and heading out the door.

Her inner wolf urged her on. It understood the urgency of the events happening in Blackstone.

"I know," she said as she took the stairs two at a time, not bothering to wait for the elevator. With her shifter speed, she made the trip to the garage in less than five minutes. She couldn't waste a single second. Blackstone was in danger, and they needed everyone's hands on deck.

She dashed toward the bright yellow vintage Mustang parked at the end. It was her brother Nathan's car, as was the loft she was currently staying in now. He had given it to her for safe keeping. "No, Kate, I'm not giving her to you," Nathan had said when she asked if she could keep the car. "And you better take care of her!"

Hmmph. As if she couldn't. While she may not have had Nathan or their father's mechanical know-how, she knew how to respect a car, especially a classy piece like the 'Stang. Her dad promised her they'd fix up a car for her too, once him and Ma were back from their retirement trip this year. She couldn't wait as she had already began researching what she wanted. Maybe a Chevelle or a Charger. Electric blue, with a stripe down the middle. She could dye her hair to match, too. But that would have to wait since she needed to pony up the cash first. House sitting for Nathan and Violet helped cut her bills, but she had a long way to go.

For now at least, she could have the pleasure of driving

this baby. As she turned the key in the ignition and pressed her foot on the gas, she could hear and feel the power of the engine. The vibrations sent a thrill through her. *Even better than sex*, she thought as she put the car in reverse and backed out of the parking spot.

Not that she'd had any earthshaking experiences lately. When was the last time …? She didn't even want to think about it. Too long. *Does your hooha close up when you don't use it?* Maybe save that one for a Google search later.

She floored it the entire drive, making it to the Lennox Corp. Headquarters in no time, waving at Jenkins the security guard who recognized her and opened the gates as she approached.

As soon as she parked, she whipped her phone out to text Sybil Lennox, her best friend, who was already at Lennox Corp. However, when she heard the flapping of wings and the loud thud as the ground shook, she put the phone away and got out of the car.

A large, twenty-foot dragon had landed in the parking lot, dropping off two figures she recognized as Luke Lennox and —*Thank Jeebus*—little Grayson Mills. From what she'd heard, the bad guys had kidnapped him and his mother. Luke and Sybil must have found him. But where was Georgina Mills? As the dragon flew off, the two dashed through the doors of the main building. Sybil would tell her.

Kate rushed in their direction but slowed down as she got closer to the entrance. As she predicted, seconds later, Sybil Lennox walked around from behind the Lennox Headquarters building, buttoning up her blouse.

"Where have you been?" Sybil admonished as her silvery gray eyes landed on Kate. "I've been texting and calling all morning!"

"I know, I know!" She put her hands up. "Mr. Douchenozzle McDickbag kept me on the phone."

"Martin Dennis again?" Sybil asked as they entered the glass doors and walked to the elevators. "What was the matter *this time*?"

Kate rolled her eyes. "What *isn't* the matter? I can't seem to please the guy. I think it's because he wants my contract to go to his son. Some programmer bro who just got out of college." She huffed and watched as the numbers on the elevator display ascended. "Anyway, catch me up to speed."

As they made their way to the fifteenth floor, Sybil explained what had happened after their friend Georgina and her bear cub, Grayson, were kidnapped. The boy was somehow able to escape their captors, and he found a way to get help and get in contact with them. Sybil and her brother Luke had just arrived from picking him up. Georgina, however, was still with the captors.

"Those sons of bitches!" Kate said.

"We'll find her," Sybil reassured her. "We have to."

The elevator halted, signaling their arrival at the secret headquarters of the The Shifter Protection Agency or simply, The Agency. There was a flurry of activity everywhere, and one of the agents pointed them toward the glass office in the corner. When they walked in, Kate realized that everyone was already there. Like, *everyone*, including Ma, Pop, Nathan, and Violet, who had flown in from out of the country. *Shit*.

"Sorry we're late!" Kate rushed in, not waiting for Sybil. "Motherfuckin' client wouldn't let me off the phone. Kept on and on about how he hated the GUI I made. I told him to stick it up his ass and—"

Holy fuck.

It was like she ran into an invisible solid brick wall, the

force nearly knocking her back. But it wasn't a wall. No, it was a pair of eyes the color of the sea that seemed to have had her pinned in place. They bore right into her. His handsome face remained passive, but his nostrils flared.

Mine, her wolf whined.

And his wolf. Oh wow. It roared back so wild and strong that it pushed at her like a wave.

"Petros?" Christina Lennox, head of the The Shifter Protection Agency in Blackstone, said. "You were saying?"

He broke his gaze, turning away from her. "Yes. I mean …."

Everyone's attention went back to him as he spoke. And why wouldn't it? This was life and death after all. It was a good thing too, because then she could ogle him without anyone noticing. She couldn't help it. He was so gorgeous, almost *too* gorgeous. His hair was dark as midnight, and his shoulders were broad and wide. The black shirt he wore clung to his well-developed muscles, and whorls of ink snaked out from under the sleeves. The fabric was so tight, she could see the outline of his abs. His olive skin was tanned, and she wondered if he was the same color all over—

"Kate!" Sybil hissed beside her, nudging her. "Are you listening?"

"Huh? Yeah!" Of course she was listening to him. How could she not? That damn accent was sexy, and the vibrations of his low voice sent heat straight to her core.

Mine!

Her wolf said it so loudly this time, she feared he heard it. And it was like he did, because those blue-green eyes flicked back at her. Her own wolf whimpered and turned, raising its hind quarters to—

Stop it, bitch!

Oh no. This couldn't be. This gorgeous, over six feet of

hunky deliciousness with the bangin' bod couldn't be her mate.

Mine.

No no no! There was some mistake. They hadn't even been introduced. And she didn't *want* a mate. Her life was fine just the way it was. She did what she wanted, whenever she wanted. Hell, she did *who* she wanted, though at this moment the thought of being with any other man made her mouth turn to dust.

No. Absolutely not.

They would have a serious discussion about this. Maybe he didn't want a mate, either. He was hot; she bet all the girls threw themselves at him. Why would he want to tie himself down?

Mine, her wolf growled.

Bitch.

Yes, they would have a calm, adult discussion. Of course, not right now. Maybe later, when they saved Blackstone and her panties weren't on fire just looking at him, they would both realize they couldn't possibly be mates.

"So," Christina began, "I'll start assigning teams of two to lead volunteers—"

"I'm going with Vi!" Kate announced, stomping over to her brother's mate.

The tiger shifter's light blue eyes widened with surprise. "Me?"

"What?" Nathan groused. "She should be with me."

"You've had her all to yourself for weeks," Kate pointed out.

"But—"

"Shush!" She looped her arm through Violet's. "It's settled."

The moment Christina finished her briefing with everyone, Kate practically dragged Violet out of the office.

"So," Violet began, "how is everything?"

"Good," Kate said, glancing around them. "I mean, you know, aside from the whole 'our enemies planted bombs all over the place to kill us all' thing. And you? How are the orphans? Anything new?"

Violet gave her a knowing smile. "The girls are healthy and happy. And as for something new," she lowered her voice, "I'm pregnant."

"What?" Kate stopped in her tracks. "Oh my God! Who else knows?"

"Just your mother and father. They were planning to visit us next week with my parents, but we had to tell them as soon as we got here," Violet said.

"Oh my God!" She wrapped Violet in a tight hug. "I'm so happy for you guys! I'm going to be an Auntie!"

"Yes, happy news, for sure." Violet rubbed her stomach. "And well, maybe a cousin to follow soon for my little one?"

"Huh?" Kate feigned. "You know what? I think it doesn't make sense for us to be partners—" She tried to turn and get away, but Violet's grip on her arm was too strong, plus Kate would never push a pregnant broad.

"That wolf is your mate."

"Who?"

The tiger shifter crossed her arms over her chest. "You know who. The big, surly-looking guy. I know the look that passed between you two."

Damn. Violet was too smart for her own good. "It's not what you think," Kate said. "I don't even know him. We might not be compatible."

"Well, then, you'll have to get to know him. Don't tell Nathan I said so, but that Greek wolf is hot."

"Greek?"

"Yes, he's from Lykos."

"Oh." So he came here with Ari Stavros all the way from Greece. Which meant he wouldn't be staying too long. She convinced herself that was for the best.

"Speaking of which." Violet nodded her head to the left.

Kate turned her gaze down the hall and swallowed a big lump in her throat. The Greek wolf was stalking toward them, his large body tense as he walked with slow, lumbering steps. She found herself paralyzed by his gaze again, and it was only when Violet kicked her shin that she was able to move her limbs. By this time, he was already inches away from her. He raised an arm toward her.

"You are—"

"Sorry, gotta go!" Kate said, ducking under his massive bicep. "I think I hear Sybil calling me!" She waved as she dashed down the hallway.

She turned the corner, listening for footsteps behind her, but it seemed he didn't follow her. Placing a hand over her hammering heart, she calmed herself. *Okay*, she thought, *all I have to do is avoid him until he leaves*. Or, rather, first, save the town while avoiding him. *Easy peasy*. She was a master at avoiding responsibility all her life; she could escape one wolf for a few hours.

"Oh God," Kate exclaimed as she watched Uncle Hank transform from a giant fire-breathing dragon into his human form. "We did it."

Blackstone was saved. Thanks to the people who stayed behind to look for the bombs planted by The Organization, they were able to find all the explosives and disable their remote detonation devices. The Chief, their leader, tried to set them off manually, but Luke and Uncle Hank had stopped them.

Relief swept through her, and as the adrenaline left her body, her shoulders sagged. She had spent the last few hours combing every inch of her assigned quadrant for bombs with her partner, Kendra Johnson, a female officer from Blackstone P.D. They found two right behind Rosie's Cafe and Bakeshop and had quickly called it in so they could be diffused. They were guarding the bombs, making sure none of the goons from The Organization could get to them, when they heard the sound of gunshots coming from Main Street.

Kate ran out and saw everything—how Uncle Hank had swooped down to protect Luke with his bulletproof body. When fire and lava spewed from his mouth, the heat was nearly unbearable, and Kate covered her face with her arm.

But now, it was over. And everything would be fine. Oh, and it looked like Luke and Georgina were reuniting. They were embracing and—

"You have been avoiding me."

Oh crap.

Slowly, she pivoted on her heel. "I wouldn't call it avoiding as much as, uh, giving us some space."

Ocean-colored eyes stared down at her. "I do not need any space from you, *mate*."

"Wait!" She raised her hands as he approached her.

He stopped. "Yes?"

"Well, I—oh look over there! I think there's a bomb!" She pointed behind him, and he turned his head. While he was distracted, she took her chance and made a mad dash for the opposite direction.

Ha! That stu—"Hey! What the fuck?"

The entire world turned upside down. Oh no, wait, it wasn't the world. It was her. That cocky bastard had her over his shoulder and was now carrying her away to God knows where.

"Put me down, you—you—*caveman*!" she screamed at him. "What the hell do you think you're doing?" She kicked her legs and beat her fists down his broad back, but he didn't even flinch.

All her blood rushed to her head, and she lost all sense of thought. Yeah, that was probably why she was staring at his ass instead of trying to fight him off. And oh *fucking hell*, he smelled good. Hmmm ... like the sea, clean and fresh with just a hint of sweat. Her wolf was going crazy, urging her to touch him.

She yelped when he finally put her upright. Where the hell were they? Glancing around, she saw they were in the empty parking lot behind the bookshop on Main Street. The blood draining out of her head made her dizzy, and she stepped back, bracing herself against the solid wall behind her.

"Are you all right?" he asked, his voice suddenly gentle.

"I'm fine!" she said. "No thanks to you. How could you do that? Carrying me off like some troglodyte?"

"A what?"

"You know. Caveman. Sticks and rocks. Fire. Cave paintings."

He gave her a puzzled look. "English is not my first language, but I will take note and Google it later."

"Yeah, you do that." She tried to turn away from him, but

he placed his arm across her, planting his palm on the wall to stop her.

"You are my mate," he said. "You must have felt it. Heard our wolves call to each other. I've searched for so long ... I thought I would never find you. You're more exquisite than I could have imagined."

His words sent a shiver through her, and her knees wobbled like jelly. He thought she was exquisite? She couldn't remember any man ever saying that to her. Maybe hot. And sexy. And that they liked her small tits. But not *exquisite*, like she was something to be worshipped and cherished forever, not just for a couple hours of fun.

No! This wasn't right! This wasn't how it was supposed to be. This was too much. "Look, uh, what's your name again?"

"Petros Thalassa."

"Right. Petros." She put a hand on his chest. Jeez, it was like a rock. "This isn't how we do things in America."

"I know, but you wouldn't—"

"Look, I don't believe in mates."

"You do not?"

She shook her head. "I believe in choices. I'm a modern woman, you know? And I believe we should have a choice in who we spend the rest of our lives with, or if we even choose to do that at all."

His jaw set. "I would never force myself on you."

"What? Oh, I'm not talking about *that*." Of course, her dirty, dirty mind immediately went to *that,* and she was pretty sure there wouldn't be any need for force. "Look, I'm sure you're a great guy, Petros. I'm just not looking for anyone right now, ya know? My life is fine the way it is."

"But we are mates," he said. "Fated to be together, me and you ... uh ..." His brows knitted together.

"Kate," she supplied, rolling her eyes.

"Kate." He gave a nod. "A beautiful name. Like you."

"Uh, thanks?"

He reached down and wrapped his large hands around her wrists, the touch sending a zing of electricity across her skin. "Kate-mine, you are a worthy mate," he said. "And you will be a strong mother to our pups—"

"Just hold on a minute!" she cried, struggling to raise her hands. "Did you not understand a single word I said? About not looking for anyone right now?"

He nodded. "Of course you are not looking for anyone. I am already here."

"That's not—"

But she didn't get a chance to finish her sentence as he pulled her to him and his lips landed on hers.

Holy. Mother. Of. God.

When she was sixteen, Kate once picked up one of those trashy romance novels Sybil used to read and was so bored by the descriptions that she threw it away. It sounded trite. Trumpets and angels singing in the background? Shivers down the spine? Feeling breathless? It sounded like a load of bull crap, and no boy she ever kissed before that and since then made her feel that way.

But this *kiss*? Oh fuck.

Petros' lips were warm against hers, rough and demanding, coaxing her to respond. Kate realized he let go of her wrists, so she wound her arms around his neck to pull him down closer. His body slammed against hers, pushing her up against the wall and trapping her there. That fucking amazing tongue of his snaked inside her mouth, tangling with her own. He tasted like the sun and the ocean and the earth ... she couldn't describe it, but that was the closest thing she could think of. Inside her, her wolf howled in delight.

Hands moved down from her waist, over her ass, and under her knees. He lifted her up and wrapped her legs around his waist. Fucking hell, she could feel the significant bulge of his cock rubbing right against her. Right *there*. Her panties were soaked through in an instant. He was perfectly lined up against the seam of her pussy, like he knew just how to position his body to send tingles of pleasure all over her. Oh God, she was going to come, right out here in the open, riding Petros as he continued to rub himself on her.

"Ahem."

They both froze, and while Kate's arms fell down to her side, Petros didn't move and kept her pinned against the wall.

"I hate to interrupt ... whatever this is," Jason Lennox said in a wry voice. "But we've still got work to do."

Petros cleared his throat, unwound her legs from his waist, then set her down. He turned around. "Of course. Apologies. We were carried away."

"From what I heard, you were the one doing the carrying away." Jason looked at Kate. "Kate, are you ... okay? Do you need me to—"

Petros stepped in front of her. "Of course she is okay. She is my mate."

"Oh." Jason sounded relieved. "Well, I guess I can tell Christina to give you five more minutes."

"Wait!" Kate called, but Jason was already gone. She looked at Petros and then smacked him on the arm. *Ouch, that hurt.* "Why did you say that to him?"

"Because it is the truth."

"But that's not ... you can't ... that's not the point!" She let out a frustrated sound.

"What does it matter? Soon everyone will know," he said matter-of-factly.

"Arggh!" She stamped her foot in irritation. "You stubborn wolf! Why won't you listen to me?"

He placed a hand on her shoulder. "Kate-mine, I am listening to you. To your wolf. It wants me as much as you do."

"Gah!" she choked in anger. She wanted to deny it, but for some reason she couldn't make the words come out of her mouth. "I can't do this! You … you stay away from me! Go back to Lykos!"

"But—"

She waved a hand at him. "I swear to God, you come near me and you'll regret it!"

Petros' face turned stormy, but he nodded. "I will leave you be for now. Perhaps you need some time to come to your senses." He turned those intense blue-green eyes back at her. "But know this: you cannot stop fate."

She stared after him as he walked away. The wind whooshed right out of her lungs, and it was hard to breathe. His words rang in her head. They sounded like a promise. No, they were a threat.

Oh yeah? Well, she didn't do well when she was threatened. *I'll show you, asshole.* Oh no, she was not going to just bend over to fate. She would fight it kicking and screaming.

CHAPTER ONE

"And we're one hundred percent sure that all the bombs have been found and disabled?" Christina Lennox asked.

"Yes," Petros Thalassa replied as he reached over and switched off the projector that flashed a map of Blackstone on the screen behind him. The conference room went dark for a second before the lights flickered back on. "We used the tech your father brought over from Lykos to sweep the entire town. All the detonation devices have also been destroyed, so there's no chance of anyone setting them off."

"All right." Christina turned toward her team. "Just to let you know, The Chief and everyone we rounded up in the attack are now in the custody of the federal government. The attorney general himself has assured us that they will prosecute to the full extent of the law. Our own attorneys will be working with them to ensure they face the harshest punishment possible. That is why anything solid we can offer them will be of the utmost importance."

Petros nodded. "We have already begun cataloging the evidence."

"Good job everyone." Christina gathered her things. "Let's finish up our reports and have them sent back to Lykos by end of day. Dismissed."

All the people in the meeting stood up from their chairs and began to gather their things. The conference room began to empty, but as Petros was about to leave, he stopped when he heard Christina call his name.

"Petros, one moment please," she said as she walked over to his end of the conference table. She sat in one of the empty chairs and motioned for him to take the one in front of her. "I need to speak with you."

"Of course Miss—I mean, Christina." The name felt strange on his tongue; she'd been Miss Stavros to him all his life. There was a pack hierarchy after all, even on Lykos, and it was not proper for someone like him to call the Alpha's adopted daughter by her given name. Even when they worked together as agents, he called her that. But once he arrived in Blackstone, she insisted he call her by her given name. "What can I do for you?" he said as he sat down.

"Well, I just wanted to see how you were doing." She shifted in her seat. "I mean, adjusting to life here in Blackstone."

"It's very different," he said. "Everything is different. Even the landscape. It's all green and lush."

"I know," she replied, a wistful look on her face. "I miss the sea sometimes."

"I would expect that." His jaw hardened as he ground his teeth together.

She turned her light blue eyes at him, giving him a knowing gaze. Christina Stavros—Lennox, he corrected—was much smarter than people gave her credit for. It was not a surprise her father, Ari Stavros, Head of The Shifter Protection Agency, gave her the assignment to lead this branch. "I was very surprised when Father said he was sending you here to be my lieutenant. And that you had volunteered to come here."

"You were?"

"You hardly leave Lykos, except for missions," Christina pointed out. "Have you ever gone on vacation anywhere? Or even traveled to the mainland?"

"What for?" he asked. "We had everything we needed on Lykos."

"So, why come here?" she asked. "Was it because of what happened in Cyprus?"

Petros' body went involuntarily still, and the tension in the room became thick as syrup. The memory was still so clear in his mind, and he thought of it every day. About what he could have done differently. If he wasn't so good at compartmentalizing, he would have gone truly mad months ago.

Christina leaned forward and placed her hands on the conference table. "You know, no one blames you for—"

"It's not about that," he interrupted, trying to drive the memories away. They were still too fresh, even after all these months, that he could relive it if he ever let his thoughts stray toward that dark path. He clenched his jaw.

"So, if it's not that, what made you want to leave Lykos now?"

The question caught him off guard, and he remained silent for a few seconds. "Those reasons are my own. It will not affect the way I do my job, I assure you."

Blue eyes widened in surprise, but Christina regained her composure. "Of course. I didn't mean to pry. You are allowed your privacy and reasons."

"Thank you." He stood up, despite it being rude to not wait

until she did. But the conference room felt stuffy and constricted at the moment. "If there's nothing else, I would like to head back to my hotel."

"Yes. I mean, wait. There is." She stood up and walked over to him. "She'll be at The Den tonight."

"Pardon me?"

She gave him a smirk. "Kate. She'll be at this bar called The Den. Just at the edge of town."

He thought about playing dumb, but no, Christina Lennox was smart, and he did not want to insult her. He gave her a grateful nod. "Thank you for the information."

"Kate is ... special," Christina said.

"I know."

"Not just because she's your mate," she added. "I mean, you may need some special handling in her case." She gave a little laugh. "Frankly, I'm surprised, but then again, not. I like to think that fate brings us to the person who needs us most."

"My mate does not seem needy," he pointed out.

Christina patted him on the shoulder. "I wasn't talking about *her*. Good night, Petros."

"Good night, Christina."

Petros closed up the conference room and shut the door behind him. As he walked out of the Lennox Corp. building, he looked around. Christina was right, about Blackstone being so different from Lykos. And that was a good thing.

Even though he wasn't born there, Lykos was all Petros ever knew. He knew every person, every rock, every tree, and every grain of sand. But there was one thing he was sure of, something that had been on his mind for the last few years: his mate was not there. The woman the universe intended him to be with forever was somewhere out there, and if he stayed on the island, he might never meet her.

Besides, there was nothing left there. Sure, despite his background, he had risen up the ranks. Who could have guessed that someone like him would someday become the right-hand man to the Alpha's daughter? Not the people of Lykos, not even the couple who raised him, that was for sure.

As Petros slipped into the driver's seat of his rented pickup truck, he paused, placing his hands on the wheel. He thought being out in the world might give him a better chance of finding his mate, of finally having a family, and finding a home—a real one—his heart had yearned for all these years.

But, he never expected *her*.

Sure, his wolf, wild and feral that it was, had recognized her instantly. And she was more beautiful than he could have ever imagined, than he could ever deserve. Green eyes like emeralds that shifted shades when she was amused or angry. Dark blonde hair that cascaded down her back like a waterfall, with dyed pink ends that suited her. Even the tiny, sparkling jewel on her nose added to her exotic beauty. And that body—lithe and graceful. He longed to have her underneath him or over him as they made love, and then see her belly ripe with their pup. No, he didn't expect Kate Caldwell at all.

Or her reluctance.

His wolf growled at him angrily. Like it was *his* fault. The wolf wanted her badly, to mate with her and be with her. The funny thing was his animal was aware it was damaged, but it so desperately wanted to be fixed. Petros knew his lonely heart and broken wolf needed a mate. And perhaps, just maybe, he'd finally find some peace and forgiveness for his transgressions.

But why she acted that way, he did not know. He had very little experience with women, and none at all with romantic relationships. She said she needed space, and he gave it to her, but he was done waiting like some fool. They were mates, and he would make her see reason.

Reaching over to the GPS unit on the dash, he typed in "The Den." After a few seconds of calculating, the screen lit up with the map and the way to the bar. To his destiny.

The Den was not too far out from the center of town. Petros parked the truck in the one remaining slot at the end of the lot, cut off the engine, and made his way inside.

It was a Friday night, which explained why it was so crowded. His wolf bristled at all the people. It hated crowds, and all the shifters in here didn't make it any better. He'd been surrounded by wolves all his life and being around so many different animals was unnerving. A few of them gave him strange looks as he passed by, probably sensing his agitated animal.

Calm down, he urged the wolf. *No one is here to harm you.*

He walked around, his eyes searching for his mate. Although this seemed like a decent establishment, he did not like how there were so many males in here. Bears, wolves, tigers, stags, even a flight shifter or two ... he didn't care for so many unattached shifters congregating in a place his mate apparently frequented.

"What can I get ya, honey?" The blonde bartender asked as he approached the bar.

"I don't suppose you have any *grappa*?" he asked.

She frowned at him. "What's that? A fancy cocktail or somethin'?"

"Never mind. A beer, please."

"Coming right up." She grabbed a glass from the shelf, filled it up from the tap, and slid it toward him. He took it with a grateful nod and dropped a bill on the table. "Keep the change."

She did a double-take when she saw the bill's denomination. "Oh. You sure? Thanks!"

He took a sip of the cold brew, then looked back across the bar. Where could she be?

"And then I told him to go fuck a trumpet!"

Ah, there she was. He would recognize her anywhere, as the sound of her beautiful voice was unmistakable. It called to him, even with the din in the room. He followed the foul-mouthed diatribe until it led him to a table in the corner occupied by three females.

"You didn't really say that, did you Kate?" one of the girls asked.

"Of course I did," she said smugly. "I'm Kate *motherfucking* Caldwell."

"Ladies," he greeted them.

Kate's back was to him, but he could see her body tense. She turned slowly, her brows drawn together. He longed to kiss away that wrinkle between them. "What the hell are you doing here?"

"I was told you would be here, and so I thought I'd come."

"Why?"

"Why?" he asked, his voice raising. "To see you. Because you're my m—"

She slapped her hand over his mouth. "Shush!"

"You know half the town already knows, right?" The dark-haired girl sitting on the stool rolled her eyes. Petros recognized her as Sybil Lennox, youngest of the Lennox dragons. "You know, after he threw you over his shoulder, caveman style, and took you behind the book shop for a make-out session?"

"I have Googled this 'caveman' you talk about," Petros said. "I know what you mean now. But from my research, it seems more appropriate if I dragged you by your hair." He frowned. "Which I would never do."

"Yeah, but you've manhandled me, right?" Kate asked.

"You didn't seem to mind me 'handling' you. You are my ma—"

"I said shush!" She looked around. "People are going to hear."

"And why shouldn't they hear?" Petros said. "Everyone needs to know you are spoken for." Petros knew half the men in the room had been eyeing the three lone females. Oh, they could stare all they want at the two other women, but Kate was *his*. His wolf gnashed its teeth in agreement.

"Oh my," the other female, a petite redhead, fanned her face. "It's getting way too hot in here. Shall we go for some air, Sybil?"

"Great idea, Dutchy," the female dragon said, slipping off the stool. "You two have fun." She winked at Kate as they left.

"I was trying to have a nice girls' night with my friends." She took the bottle of tequila on the table, filled up a shot glass, then knocked it back. "And now you've driven them away. Who am I supposed to talk to about my problems?"

"Me, of course," he said matter-of-factly. Yes, from now on, they would tell each other their thoughts and lean on each other in times of need. "Now, tell me: what is troubling you?"

She shot him a suspicious look but seemed to relent. "I just lost a client. A big one."

"Oh." He realized that aside from her name, he knew very little about his mate. "So, you are lacking funds, then?" If she needed money, she could have all of his. He would never let anything happen to her, of course.

"What?" She looked at him like he had grown a second head on his shoulder. "No. I mean, I still have Lennox as a main client, plus I can always take on more projects to pay the bills. This client ... one of the managers has been on my ass for months, trying to get me fired. And they finally did it when I couldn't deliver some changes on time."

"They have not been treating you well, then. So it's not such a loss, maybe?"

She took another shot of tequila. "That's not the point, Petros."

"I'm confused."

"Barkley Industries was my first client," she explained. "The one I got all by myself, without any help from my family."

"You are vexed because your family has been helping you?" Now he was really confused. His mate had a family, and yet she spurns their help?

"Yes!" she said. "Finally, you understand."

"Actually, I do not." Never mind. His mate was in distress. She needed a solution. "Well, it sounds as if you are upset with losing this client of yours. I suggest you go and search for other clients, send your CV to—"

"Argh!" She grabbed the bottle and drank straight from it. "Are you seriously giving me advice?"

"Is that not the point of this?" he asked, gently taking the bottle away from her. "To talk and find a solution?"

"Oh my God. You are such a man!" She tried to swipe the bottle back, but he held it high above her. "No. The point of this, of having a girls' night, is so I can vent about Douchenozzle McDickbag and get drunk!"

Women were confusing. Normally, had it been any other

person, he would have walked away. But this was his mate, and thus he needed to comfort her. Besides, she looked absolutely adorable as she jumped up and down, trying to grab the bottle of liquor from his outstretched arm. He placed the bottle down on the tray of a passing waitress and then turned to her, placing his hands on her arms to calm her. "Tell me what I need to do then, Kate-mine."

"First off, you need to stop calling me that," she hissed.

"But you are Kate," he leaned down and whispered in her ear. "And you are definitely mine." He felt her shiver at his words and her guard lowering. Feeling bold, he pressed his lips to the spot where her neck met her shoulder. This time, she let out a soft gasp. He pressed his nose against the pulse under her ear. Her scent was incredible—like pine trees and earth and fresh mountain air. So different and wild, just like her.

"Shit," she cursed, and then pulled away before he could move his lips up to hers. "We can't—" She pushed him away. "Look, it's not you, it's me, okay?" She took a deep breath. "I'm just not mate material. Hell, I'm not even relationship material." She took the purse hanging from the back of one of the chairs and slung it over her shoulder.

"Where are you going?" he asked.

"Home." She pointed a finger at him. "And don't even think of following me, or I'm going to call the cops and have you arrested for stalking."

His mate sounded serious. "I will never harm you, Kate-mine."

"I told you to—never mind!" She pivoted and walked away.

Petros watched his mate as she made her way across the room and out the door. Why did she keep resisting the pull of their animals?

He realized he did not know anything about mates. His "parents," after all, had never taught him about mates before they died. Or any other life lessons, for that matter. But he tried not to be bitter because the past was past.

Perhaps mating was not as easy as he thought it was, and he needed to put in more effort instead of expecting her to fall at his feet. Hmm … his mate wanted to be chased, huh? Well, he always knew nothing worth having came easy, and his Kate was worth more than anything in the world.

CHAPTER TWO

Kate rolled over on the mattress, taking the sheets with her. She let out a long sigh as she opened her eyes. *Should have had more tequila.* It took a lot to get her drunk, though. She wondered how much it would take to make her forget about Petros. Maybe she should call up a tequila factory in Mexico and see if they delivered by the truckload.

"Argh!" Even in sleep, she couldn't get rid of him. Her dreams were filled with that infuriating wolf. His lips, those eyes, that hot bod. More specifically, being under that body. And she could listen to his voice over and over again. Low and growly, and God, that accent. She'd heard people with accents before, but Petros' was the only one that threatened to melt her panties off.

If she wasn't a shifter, she was pretty sure she'd have carpal tunnel syndrome by now from all the times she'd diddled herself since she met him. Even now, she could feel the ache and pulsing between her legs.

Mine.

She sat up so quickly, the blood rushing to her brain made

her dizzy. "Uh, shut up!" She meant what she said to Petros last night. She was not girlfriend material; she made sure of that.

Growing up under the protective shadow of not only her older brother, but his friends, made life difficult for Kate. Her only friends growing up were Amelia and Sybil, who could relate to what she was going through. She, of course, rebelled against them, doing the opposite of what they wanted. Sneaking out at night, smoking under the bleachers, and yes, even dating the school's resident bad boy. She thought he was so cool, but little did she know that he wasn't just bad, but *really* bad.

No, don't think about that.

She'd taken care of that *jerk*. No need to dwell on the past.

Kate knew she was not someone Petros could bring home to his parents. And definitely not mate material. In any case, he didn't belong here anyway. Maybe he was sticking around while they were wrapping things up with last week's incident, but soon he'd be on his way back to his island paradise in the Mediterranean.

She ignored that tightening knot in her stomach. This was for the best.

The strong vibrations from the bedside table knocked her out of her thoughts. She frowned. Who would call her this early on a Saturday? It was—oh shit, it was nearly noon. She grabbed her phone before it danced off the table.

"Hello?"

"Kate? It's Christina."

"Hey, Chrissy," she said. She heard the soft, annoyed snort from the other woman, but she didn't care. She loved giving people nicknames, or in this case, using one that annoyed them. She remembered how stuck up Christina was when she first arrived in Blackstone. At least she had loosened up since then. "What's up?"

"Are you free for lunch?"

Lunch? Strange. Christina never sought her out before. "I guess."

"Well, I feel terrible about ignoring your texts about girls' night."

"And my emails? And my voice messages?" She really needed her girls, but she knew Christina was probably busy cleaning up after The Organization, so she wasn't too upset about her not showing up last night.

"Uh, yeah, those too." She paused. "So, how about lunch at Giorgio's? My treat."

Her stomach growled with hunger. A free lunch at the best Italian restaurant in town? What could go wrong? "Sure! I'll hop in the shower and meet you there in about thirty minutes."

Kate walked into Giorgio's at twelve-thirty on the dot, feeling famished. The smell of fresh bread and tomato sauce wafted in her nose. *Amazing.* When was the last time she'd eaten at Giorgio's? Probably during her parents' anniversary, since she didn't exactly have the budget to eat here all the time.

She scanned the room and quickly found Christina, sitting at a table by the window. She waved to Giorgio Allementari, the owner of the restaurant and pointed to her companion. The handsome and flamboyant restaurateur smiled and nodded at her as he continued to give instructions to his wait staff.

"Hello, Kate," Christina greeted and motioned to the chair

in front of her. Even on a Saturday morning she looked all business-like in a crisp white shirt and khaki pants, her blonde hair up in an elegant French twist.

"Hey, Chrissy." She plopped herself down. "What's up?"

"How was girl's night?" There was a twinkle in her eyes, something that told Kate she had something to do with Petros showing up.

"Oh you know, same old, same old." She grabbed the menu and opened it up. If Christina was buying, she should choose the most expensive things. That would show her. Not that she could ever bankrupt the heiress. "Things at The Agency keeping you busy?" *Hmm, the filet mignon? And maybe some white truffle pizza too.*

Christina's face turned serious. "Just because we got rid of The Chief doesn't mean our work is done. Which is why I called you today."

Now *this* was interesting. Kate put the menu down. "All right. Spill."

"Kate, we need your help."

"Me?" she asked, puzzled. "What can I do to help?"

"We need your skills, of course. We're so short staffed right now." She let out an exasperated sigh. "Why do you think I'm working overtime? Even on weekends?"

"I don't exactly have any super spy experience," she pointed out. "I took some self-defense classes, and I can fight as a wolf, but other than that, I don't know what I can offer."

"Well, you're a software engineer. You can help us put our systems together," Christina said. "That's what you do for Lennox, right? And at the mines?"

"Yeah, but …." Why were her instincts suddenly on red alert? She should be jumping for joy instead. After all, she just lost a client yesterday, after Douchenozzle McDickbag fired her for not delivering the changes to their app on time as she was helping save a whole town. Besides, it was technically The Agency's fault (or rather, The Organization's) that she lost her other biggest client. "I don't come cheap, you know."

"Don't I get the friends and family discount?" Christina asked.

Had she been drinking, the joke would have made Kate spit take her water.

"I'm kidding. We'll pay your usual rates," Christina said without missing a beat. "We really need all the help we can get, especially now that we have Dr. Mendle's diaries to sift through."

Dr. Mendle. The name made Kate's blood boil. He was the sick bastard who had experimented on all those shifters over the last two decades and kept Grayson Mills locked up in a cage.

"All right." How could she say no? Besides, that Chevelle on eBay she'd had her eye on had about another thirty days left on auction. If she wanted the car, she'd have to come up with the cash soon. "I'll do it."

"Great!" Christina signaled a waiter, who came by with a bottle of champagne.

Kate raised a brow. "Champagne? For lunch?"

"It *is* the weekend." Christina flashed her a sweet smile as the waiter handed her a flute. "Let's make a toast? To your—er, our union?"

She grabbed the other flute from the waiter. "Right." As she looked at Christina over the rim of her glass, she couldn't help but hear those alarm bells ringing in her head again. Still, she couldn't complain. Fate may have been a bitch to her the last week, but now it seemed she was being rewarded with another lucrative job dropping in her lap.

CHAPTER THREE

Petros walked into The Agency's headquarters at precisely eight a.m. Monday morning. Although the offices were open, the only other people there were the skeleton crew manning the overnight shift. He gave them a terse nod and headed to his office. It seemed strange to even have an office. He was not used to being in a management position, having been in the field for more than a decade.

As soon as he turned eighteen, Petros signed up to become part of The Agency. It involved six months of hard training in the most adverse conditions, and only about a quarter who join make it to the end. On Lykos, it was one of the biggest honors to be chosen by Ari Stavros himself for the most elite squad of agents, the Alpha's Team. The day he had finished his training was the best day of his life. He had dreamed of it since childhood, along with his—

He slammed the door of his office shut and sat down on the shiny new leather chair by the large, sleek glass desk. Christina mentioning Cyprus had brought back those memories. Even weeks after the incident, no one would dare mention it or even say *that* name. He had worked to forget it, keep it deep inside him, or the memories would surely drive him mad and push his wolf to the brink. Maybe that was part of the reason he came to Blackstone. To forget.

No. He came here for his destiny. And though his mate was resistant, she could not stop fate. He would bide his time; after all, he was a patient man.

"Petros," a voice called his attention. "How was your weekend?"

"I mostly slept." He didn't bother to look up from the reports he was reading since he knew who it was.

Agatha Agrippina walked into his office, her hips swaying seductively as she came closer. She was one of the more junior members of the staff, and an annoying gnat he couldn't seem to swat away lately.

"You didn't do anything fun? At all?"

When he looked up, she leaned down low, showing off the generous line of her cleavage. He quickly went back to the reports he'd been reading before she barged in. "There is no time for fun, not when there is much work to be done."

"There is always time for fun, Petros," Agatha said. "What do they say here in America? 'All work and no fun' and all that?"

With a long sigh, he put the reports down. "Why did you come into my office uninvited?" He really had no time for her games, and his patience was running short with her. Since she arrived a few days ago, she'd done nothing but pester and hover around him.

Of course, he already knew what she wanted—Agatha seemed determined to sleep her way to the top, and she wasn't shy about it. Some said she had her sights on bagging one of Ari Stavros' sons and was using her position as an agent to get close to them. She was a fool though, if she thought any of them would even consider taking her seriously. Nikos Stavros would maybe play with her, but Kostas or Xander? They were both far too serious and responsible to sleep with a member of the team. And Petros was smart enough to follow in their lead.

"I'm just making small talk. Or water cooler talk, as they say," Agatha said with a petulant pout. "You know, Blackstone has so many things to offer. There's this delightfully rustic bar called The Den—"

His wolf perked up at attention. Not because of Agatha or her insipid stories, but because *she* was here. The figure that darted into the corner of his vision moved with a familiar grace. He thought it was a mirage of some sort, but that was definitely his mate who entered through the door.

As Kate Caldwell walked into the offices of The Agency, he felt like his body had been smashed across one of the limestone cliffs back in Lykos. She looked gorgeous today, with her dark blonde and pink hair falling down in waves past her shoulders. Her skintight black leggings clung to her sexy legs, and the leather jacket she wore added a hint of danger around her. Of course, he wasn't the only one who noticed. All the male eyes around her followed her with their gaze.

Petros stood up and slammed his palms on the desk, making Agatha startle in her seat. He ignored her questions as he strode out of his office, determined to stop this nonsense.

Kate was headed toward Christina's office, unaware of the male attention. She seemed distracted in fact, and when Petros stood in her way, she didn't see him and jumped back with a small shriek.

"What the hell are you still doing here?" she asked, her pretty green eyes all ablaze.

"I live here."

"Here?" She looked around. "In the office?"

"In Blackstone."

Her jaw nearly dropped to the floor. "No, you don't."

"Yes, I do," he said. "I'm second-in-command of the Blackstone branch of The Agency. Of course I must live here now."

Her face turned red as a tomato. "That's not ... she didn't mention ... you didn't!" She clutched her laptop bag against her chest and then side stepped around him, walking straight into Christina's office.

Petros watched as Kate stormed into the glass-walled office, shutting the door behind her. As she let out what Petros presumed was a profanity-laden rant, Christina simply looked at her, cool as a cucumber, and let her continue.

He shook his head. His mate was upset, and once again it was his fault somehow. Determined to find out what happened, he walked to the office and opened the door.

Kate stood there, her face now the shade of an eggplant. Christina merely unfolded her arms and raised a brow. "Are you done? If so, maybe we can get to work."

"I'm *not* working here!" she protested.

"You signed a contract," Christina countered. "Or did you forget?"

She clenched her fists at her sides. "You sneaky ... is that why you rushed it over to me yesterday?"

"What is going on?" Petros asked, finally getting a word in.

"Great, you're here." Christina stood up and walked over to them. "Petros, meet the newest member of our team. Kate will be helping us set up and maintain our software systems."

"What?" Kate would be working here? With them? He frowned. That would definitely complicate things.

Kate huffed. "You can't force me to work here."

Christina trained her cool blue eyes on Kate. Petros expected a cutting remark, but instead she let out a long sigh. "You're right, Kate. I can't force you to do anything. You can go anytime. Petros," she said. "Kindly re-assign Adriano to keep track of the testing on the servers."

"Adriano?" Petros frowned. "But he's working on finding those trafficked shifter girls in New York. He's been tracking their movements for over 48 hours. We can't waste any time or else they could leave the country and we'll never find them."

Kate's face went red. "You're going to—" She shut her mouth and then grabbed her laptop bag. "I'll be checking over your servers and letting you know my recommendations."

The door slammed so hard, Petros feared the glass walls would shatter. He turned to Christina. "You hired her? To be part of our team?"

"Only as a contractor. She really is the best in town, and she's already familiar with the equipment Lennox bought us," Christina said. "Besides, I don't have time to hire anyone and go through the process of vetting them. And you know we can't spare anyone as it is."

He massaged the growing ache in his temple. No, this wasn't what he wanted. Having her work here would complicate things. He prided himself on being one hundred percent professional and focused. Having Kate here would be a distraction, not only to his team, but he knew he would be spending most of his time fighting off any overeager suitors.

"Petros? What's wrong?" Christina asked. "I mean, I thought this might also help you and us out. Kill two birds with one stone?"

"I'm certain Kate has killing on her mind, but it's not birds." Maybe *his* stones.

"Petros, I know we're not particularly close," Christina said. "But you helped me out a lot of times over the last year when I started as an agent. I just thought, well … if she were around more, then she could get to know you. The mate bond really is a special thing. I know you've had it rough and maybe she could—"

"It's fine," he said. Christina had thought she was helping, which made it even worse. "I'll handle it. Is there anything else?"

Christina, seemingly taking the hint, nodded her head. "Yes. I hate to dump more work on you since you're barely into your second week here, but there's another development."

"What is it?"

"My brother-in-law, Luke Lennox, will be getting married next week," Christina said. "We need to secure the event in case anyone tries to make trouble, like they did at Catherine's wedding."

"Of course," Petros said. "Once you have the details, I'll come up with a security plan."

"Thank you, Petros."

He didn't wait to be dismissed, but instead, left her office. Walking straight to the server room, he found Kate inside, a deep frown on her face as she muttered curses under her breath and examined the cabinets of computer equipment.

"It's customary for a gentleman to knock," she said without looking at him.

"I'm not a gentleman. I'm a caveman, remember?" No reaction. "Just so you know," he continued, "I did not ask her to hire you. I didn't even know you were coming here until I saw you walk in the door."

She ignored him and instead continued her perusal of the machines.

"Please, Kate-m—"

Kate whipped around to face him. "What do you want, Petros?" She stalked toward him, her steps deliberate and slow. "Do you want to fuck me? Is that it? Because if that's all you want that can be arranged—"

"I do not want a quick tumble in bed." How could she even think that? "If that were all I wanted, believe me, it would have happened already." He leaned down, staring into her eyes. "I want *you*."

"You want to own me," she shot back.

"I want you to be mine, and in turn I will be yours. I want us to share each other's lives and create a home together." He voice lowered. "And I will make love to you and give you pleasure until you beg me to stop. I want to see your belly ripen with our child."

"Ha! Ripen? Not gonna happen, dude."

"Why do you resist this?" he asked. "We are mates. Our animals call to each other. Even now, your wolf longs for me—"

"You're such a stubborn ass," she said. She straightened her shoulders. "Look, it's not you, okay? You seem like a great guy. It's *me*. I like my freedom."

"You make it sound like being mates is a trap."

"It is, isn't it?" she asked. "Besides, if you got to know me, you might not even like what you find out."

"I highly doubt that." He touched her cheek, then brushed away a lock of hair from her face. "Why would you think so?"

She planted her hands on her hips. "I'm no meek mouse who's going to bend to your every will."

"You are spirited," he said. "I know this."

"A—and I'm not just going to stay home and raise babies, if that's what you're thinking."

"We will raise them together," he said. "You could stay at home if you want, as I have a generous salary and pension from The Agency, but if your work fulfills you, then you can do that as well."

"I've been around the block a few times," she said in a defiant tone. "I'm not some virgin who—"

"You are experienced," he countered. "And you know how to please a man and will not shrink away from me."

"Are you freaking serious?" She slammed her palms on his chest. "I just told you that I've been with other m—"

The growl that came from his lips sounded feral, even to his own ears. He backed her slowly against the wall, trapping her with his body. "There will be no more talk of others. Not for me or you. I do not care about your past because all that matters is the future. From now on, it will only be you and me."

"Jesus," she muttered under her breath. "You are intense."

"I've been told I'm single-minded," he said, leaning down and tipping her face up with a finger on her chin. "But it's only with things I truly want."

"Petros."

He touched his lips to hers, gently this time. The first time they kissed had been wild and unhinged, but now he wanted slow and deliberate. He wanted to see if he had been dreaming all this time about the taste and scent of her. Oh no, it had been no dream. She was just as delicious as before, especially now as she melted against him. Finally, he was getting ahead and moving forward. She wanted him, that was for sure.

He was so wrapped up in her that he didn't hear a person

approaching the server room. It was only a split second later as the door opened that he broke away from Kate just in time.

"Petros?" Agatha's annoying nasal voice made the desire surging through his body instantly dissipate. "Where have you been? I've searched—" Her eyes narrowed as they landed on Kate. "Oh, who's your *friend*?"

Kate's face twisted. "I'm not his friend."

"No, she's not," Petros said with a smug smile. "She is my mate."

While Kate let out a choked protest, Agatha's face fell, at least for a moment. "Oh, that's nice." She flipped her hair. "Now, I need some help with those reports they need at HQ. Could you please assist me?"

"I will come to your table shortly," he said. When she didn't move, he crossed his arms over his chest. "Now go."

"Fine," she said with a pout, then pivoted on her heel and left the room.

"Why don't you go 'assist' her?" Kate spat.

He chuckled. "Green is a good look on you, my mate."

"I—what?" She pushed at him. "I'm not jealous!"

"There is no need to be jealous." Her antics amused him so much, he couldn't help himself. He placed a reassuring hand on her shoulder. "You are the only woman for me."

"Just go," she said.

Her resistance was puzzling, especially since he could feel her wolf's desire for the mating. But, then again, Kate was still a woman first. Petros reminded himself that he should not expect her to fall at his feet just because they were mates.

He had to woo her still. Having her here was a setback, as he did not want any hint of impropriety at The Agency, but hopefully since he already laid his claim to her as his mate, the others wouldn't see it that way. Christina, after all, worked with her dragon mate side by side, and no one batted an eyelash. Yes, it would not be inappropriate at all.

"I shall leave you to your work, then," he said. As he left, his mind kept going back to how he was going to win her affections. It wasn't like Lykos was an isolated island and growing up, they had access to the Internet. He had watched a lot of American movies over the years, though mostly it was action movies. He had seen a few romantic ones. Perhaps she was expecting some type of wooing in the style she was more accustomed to. If so, that was something he could definitely do.

CHAPTER FOUR

KATE HADN'T SEEN or heard from Petros in the last couple of hours as she finished her assessment of the servers. She should be glad, really. Instead, she was thinking of the skanky she-wolf who was practically eye-fucking him from three feet away.

Mine, her wolf growled possessively.

"Arrghh!" She shoved her laptop into her bag and zipped it up. Petros was free to do what he wanted and who he wanted. But the thought of him and that—that big-tittied ho-bag in bed was making her blood boil.

Kate left Lennox Corp., not bothering to stop by Christina's office or say goodbye to anyone. She would write up her recommendations tonight, and she wouldn't have to come back to implement them until they were approved, which usually took a few days, if not weeks.

Which was why she was quite surprised to get a reply from Christina an hour after she sent the email, saying everything looked good and she could start working on it the next day.

Motherfucker.

Since she didn't have any other clients right now, and she had to check in on the Lennox systems anyway, she headed straight into The Agency HQ again the following day. *Just think of the Chevelle*, she told herself. The check for the down payment she had asked for would be cleared by the end of the day. She could at least confidently put a bid on the car.

She entered the office using her ID badge and walked to the row of cubicles on the right. Christina said she could use the empty desk at the end, the one nearest to the server room.

"Who the hell is holding a funeral in here?" she exclaimed as the scent of flowers hit her nose. "What the fuck?"

On top of what was supposed to be an empty desk was a large vase of flowers. For a second, she thought she was in the wrong place. But she had a sinking suspicion of what this was. Grabbing the card, she read the contents and nearly crumpled it in her hands. "Beautiful flowers for a beautiful woman," it read, and she nearly wanted to gag.

She looked around, hoping no one would see, but it was too late. Half the office had poked their heads above their cubicle walls and was staring at her. When she turned to them with a steely expression, they all disappeared like prairie dogs going back to their hidey-holes.

With a frustrated sigh, she took the vase, walked over to the ladies' room, and dumped the flowers into the toilet and the vase in the trash. She thought about going to Petros and giving him a piece of her mind, but he wasn't in his office. She sulked back to her desk and sat down to get some work done. Opening her laptop, she put her headphones on and blasted some classic rock tunes, her favorite whenever she needed to get shit done and get lost in her work.

Kate was so deep into her coding that she didn't realize

there was someone standing next to her and nearly fell out of her chair when she felt a tap on her shoulder.

"Jeebus motherfuckin' bitchtits!" She glared at the pimply young man wearing the uniform of a well-known delivery service. "Kid, how'd you get in here?" Wasn't this a fucking *secret* headquarters?

The kid gulped visibly. "Sorry ma'am!" His voice broke. "I mean, you're Miss Caldwell, right?"

"Yeah?"

"Sign here, please." He handed her a clipboard.

With a shrug, she scrawled her name on the receipt. "Now what—"

"Here you go!" He took a box from the large satchel over his shoulder. "Enjoy."

"Enjoy?" She stared down at the heart-shaped box. "What the hell?" The white card on top read, "Sweets for my sweet."

She ripped the top of the box. *Chocolates?* They smelled really good too, not like the stale boxes you'd pick up at a gas station. These were the expensive kind of chocolates. She turned the box over. These were Belgian chocolates. Like, legit ones *from Belgium.*

This was insane. It probably cost an arm and a leg to get these here. She wanted to toss the box like she did the flowers, but she put it aside instead. She'd bring it to him later and tell him to shove it where the sun don't shine.

Kate put her headphones back on and went back to work. The sooner she finished this job the sooner she could get that fat paycheck in her pocket and get out of here.

The moment the clock struck five, she packed up her stuff. No way was she staying here. She got lucky today, with Petros not even being in the office today, but he could show up any minute.

Kate walked out of the elevator and to the employee parking lot in the front of the building. As she strode to her car, she stopped when she saw what was sitting on the hood of the Mustang. She froze as the blood roaring in her ears nearly deafened her.

The teddy bear with the red ribbon around its neck seemed innocuous enough. But the sight of it made her mind jolt back to the past. To that time she'd rather forget. This was the same tactics *he'd* use on her. To manipulate her and then make her feel guilty.

Kate took a deep breath, trying not to let the memories overwhelm her. She strode to the car, grabbed the toy, and threw it to the ground.

"Was the gift not to your liking?"

She whipped around. Petros was standing there, staring at her like an idiot. "What the fuck are you doing here?"

"I was out with my agents, securing the perimeter around Blackstone today," he explained. "I thought I would give you some space."

"Space?" she asked in an incredulous tone. She picked up the teddy bear. "You call the flowers, the chocolate, and this," she flung the offending stuffed animal at him, "space?"

Petros tossed the bear aside with a flick of his wrist before it hit his head. "What is wrong, Kate-mine? Did I offend you with my gifts?"

The anger bubbling inside her was now threatening to boil over. "Offend me? You really are a jerk! I told you to stop it with this shit!"

"Kate—"

She didn't let him get a chance to explain as she got into the Mustang, revved up the engine, and backed out of her parking space. It was a miracle she even got the car to start as her hands were shaking the entire time.

She drove away from Lennox as fast as she legally could. Nathan would kill her if she got a scratch on his car, not to mention a ticket for speeding. When she got far enough, she stopped on the shoulder of the highway, slamming the brakes so hard she heard the gravel spraying underneath the wheels.

Kate banged her forehead on the steering wheel. Did Petros realize what he'd done? By the look on his face, of course not. It was pure coincidence that he put that teddy bear on the hood of the car.

Just like what Tommy used to do.

God, she hadn't even thought of that name in years. She pushed it and the memories down, like bile threatening to rise in her throat. Sure, Tommy never touched her, but he hurt her in many other ways.

Tommy Moreau was the hottest and baddest boy in her high school. He was a coyote shifter and had transferred in from out of state for his junior year. Kate was in his math class, and she was captivated. He was handsome, and even more alluring, had a kind of danger about him. He was seventeen, and he rode a motorcycle, for Christ's sake. How could a girl resist?

They started going out immediately. At first, things were great. More than great. Kate had never felt like that before. Tommy doted on her. He *loved* her. And she thought she loved him, too. Which made her blind to everything he did.

It started with the small things. Tommy would tell her that her skirt was too short or her neckline too low. He said he couldn't concentrate when all the boys at school were looking at her. So she changed the way she dressed to please him. Then he was resentful of all the time she spent with Sybil and

Amelia, so every free moment she had was spent with him. She ignored her family and friends.

Then it started getting worse. He would call her names or tell her she looked fat in a certain outfit. When she started talking back, he would either laugh at her or accuse her of overreacting. The one time she actually had the courage to break up with him, he started shouting at her and calling her stupid and ugly. He told her she belonged to him, and no one would ever love her. They had a huge fight and she went home in tears, but the next day, as she was leaving to go to school, there was a gift on the hood of her car. A cute and cuddly teddy bear. He begged her to take him back, saying he would change. She believed him and they made up.

That's when the cycle would start all over again.

Her hands gripped the steering wheel tight. Ever since she finally broke free of Tommy's influence, she vowed to never let another man take control of her like that. No, she valued her freedom far too much, and mate or not, she would never fall into that trap ever again.

CHAPTER FIVE

PETROS WATCHED the car as it tore out of the parking lot. He let out a curse and kicked the teddy bear as he made his way to his pickup.

He managed to get into the driver's seat, despite his body feeling completely numb. Driving out of the lot, he headed back toward town, to the Blackstone Hotel where he had been staying at for the past week.

Fate really did hate him. He could confirm that now. Perhaps it was his punishment for surviving. Not just once, but twice. Because what kind of life would this be? To be living with this gigantic hole in his chest? He should have died in Cyprus. No, wait. He should have died *long* before that.

As he drove down Main Street, his stomach growled. He realized it had been hours since his last meal. Eager to get the perimeter tour done and catch Kate before she left, he had skipped lunch. Now he was famished. He was tired of eating the food at the hotel, so he decided to stop by one of the restaurants in town.

Not all the establishments were operating, though it

seemed like more and more of them were re-opening every day. There was a queue outside Rosie's Bakery and Cafe, and since patience was not part of his vocabulary at the moment, he headed to the diner instead. A friendly waitress led him to an empty table and gave him a menu.

He quickly decided on his meal and dictated his order to the young server. As he looked around, he saw someone familiar at the table across from him.

Sybil Lennox sat by herself, a book in one hand. White headphones were stuck in her ears, and she bounced her knees as she listened to some upbeat tune. Perhaps sensing Petros' gaze, she turned her silvery eyes toward him, which widened when she realized who was looking at her. She quickly put her book down, then got up and walked to his table.

"Hey! We haven't been formally introduced," she said, taking the earphones out of her ears. "I'm Sybil Lennox."

"Nice to meet you, Miss Lennox," he greeted.

"Please, it's just Sybil," she said. "And you're Petros, right?"

"Yes." He leaned back and crossed his arms over his chest. Though he was sure she was nice enough, he was not up for company at the moment.

His brusqueness didn't seem to faze her, and she flashed him a smile as she sat down on the empty chair across from him. "You know, you're not what I thought you'd be."

"Oh? And what did you think I would be?"

She chuckled. It was hard to believe this cheerful young woman housed a dangerous creature inside of her. "I mean, you're not what I thought Kate's mate would be like. She's so ... *Kate*, and you're awfully serious. But they say opposites attract, right?"

"I wouldn't know anything about that," he said glumly.

Her silver eyes sparkled. "I guess she's not making it easy for you."

"You guessed correctly."

"Don't worry," she said. "I've seen it lots of times. You can keep on resisting the mating call, but then bam!" She slapped her palms together in a dramatic manner. "You'll end up with each other anyway."

"Thank you, but I think perhaps this time fate will not be so kind." The words, once out of his mouth, weighed on his shoulders even more and the hole in his chest seemed to expand.

"What are you talking about?" Sybil asked.

Petros clasped his hands together and placed them on top of the table. "It seems no matter what I do, Kate is determined to hate me."

"What did you do?" she asked matter-of-factly.

"Excuse me?"

Sybil planted her elbows on the table and then placed her chin on her palms. "What exactly did you do?"

"Well, uh, I must admit I was too … enthusiastic the first time we met. But she was avoiding me, and I had no choice."

"No choice except to carry her off on your shoulder?" Her eyebrow raised up all the way to her hairline.

"Yes, well, perhaps that was hasty of me." He cleared his throat. "But I made my intentions clear. I'm not going to toy with her. I only wish to be with her forever and make her happy for the rest of her life."

"Did you tell her that?" Sybil asked. "I mean, did you mention that part about making her happy?"

"Er …." He scratched his head. He definitely said something about forever. And having pups with her. But for some reason, he couldn't recall telling her that all he wanted was to make her happy. But surely she must realize that, right? "I attempted to woo her today."

"Woo her?"

"Yes. I took my cues from your American movies and gave her gifts. Flowers. Chocolates. I even arranged to have a gift waiting for her on the hood of her car to surprise her."

"You did?" Sybil's eyes narrowed at him. "What kind of gift?"

"A stuffed teddy bear."

"A *what?*" Sybil rose from her seat and slammed her hands down. Petros swore he saw smoke curling out of her nostrils. The dragon inside her remained tightly reigned in, but the raw power coming from her had his own wolf frozen in apprehension. Even the other patrons stopped what they were doing to stare at them.

"A teddy—"

"I know what you said." She sank back down on the chair and placed her hands over her face. "Oh no," she said in a soft voice.

"What did I do wrong?" he asked. "Sybil?"

Putting her hands down, Sybil looked up at him, her face grim. "Look, it's not my story to tell. But … when we were younger, there was this guy. Her boyfriend. An ex."

He swallowed the jealousy rearing its ugly head. "And?"

"He didn't treat her so well."

Petros clenched his fists under the table. "Did he hurt her? Touch her?"

"What? No!" Sybil shook her head. "I would have burned him to ash if he did. He didn't hurt her physically. That was the worst part." She looked down at her shoes. "We didn't see it. None of us did." She took a deep breath. "He would make her feel bad about herself, and she would try to break up with him. Then he'd try to win her back with some kind of gift. The first one was a teddy bear, waiting for her on top of her car. Then it was other gifts. I think one time he even got her this expensive bracelet."

No wonder she had reacted that way to his gifts. It was an unfortunate coincidence, and he would most certainly not have done it had he known.

The more he thought about it, the more it made sense. Why she acted the way she did around him. His mate had been hurt in the past and having been burned, of course she would be wary of any romantic entanglement. "But she was able to get away from him."

"She did." Sybil suppressed a laugh. "And she got back at him in the most spectacular way possible. In a way only Kate could."

He breathed a sigh. At least he wouldn't have to murder anyone today. "You are her closest friend, correct?"

Sybil nodded. "She's a year younger than Amelia and me, but yeah, I've known her all my life."

"What should I do then? To win her?"

She tapped a finger on her chin. "Well, first, you need to pull back on the mate stuff. The more you make her feel trapped, the more she'll want to get away."

"Right." Okay, he could do that. Try to control his feelings of possessiveness.

"And as for the gifts ... Kate doesn't do flowers, chocolates, jewelry, and definitely no more stuffed animals."

"I think that part was made clear to me."

"Just, you know ... get to know her. Take it slow. And let her get to know you."

"Slow." It was agonizing to think he would have to take it

slow with his mate, especially when his wolf was urging him to claim her. But he would do it for her. "Okay."

Sybil clapped her hands together. "It'll work out! I know it will."

It had to work out. "Thank you, Sybil," he said.

She smiled at him, but it didn't quite reach her eyes. "Just, you know, take care of her, okay?"

"Of course." He didn't want to incur the wrath of the female dragon after all. Still, he couldn't help but notice the sadness in her eyes. "What is wrong?"

"What?" she asked. "Nothing.

"It's not nothing," Petros said. "Please, you've helped me a lot. You can confide in me as well."

Her shoulders sagged. "I'm really happy that you and Kate are mates and everything. Really, I am. It's just … well, I know that once you guys are mated and start having kids and stuff … I'll be alone."

"What?" Her words took him by surprise. "I'm not here to take Kate away from you or any of her friends."

"I know that, but … it's different. You'll see." She shifted in her seat uncomfortably. "Like, sure you guys will still be here and we'll see each other, but it will be different, you know? You'll have each other, and I'll have nobody."

"I promise you, Sybil, I will not let your friendship with Kate fade away," he said.

"That's very kind of you," she replied, seemingly mollified.

"I know all about loneliness," Petros continued. "But once you find your own mate, you won't be alone anymore."

She sighed. "Thanks, but I don't think that's ever going to happen. Everyone here is just too intimidated by who I am. And *what* I am."

Petros realized how lonely it must truly be for Sybil.

Though she was a beautiful woman, most men would be intimidated by her wealth, family, and her power. But that didn't mean her mate was not out there. He found his way to Kate, so he believed Sybil would find her intended mate, too.

"Any man who could not see past all that is a fool and not a worthy partner." He looked her straight in the eye. "Sybil, you are fierce, loyal, and strong. Any man would be lucky to have you. I have traveled many miles to meet my mate. Perhaps yours is still making his journey to you."

She gave him a weak smile. "Thank you, Petros. You're too kind. And I know you're definitely a worthy mate to Kate."

Petros hoped with his entire being that was true.

CHAPTER SIX

If Kate were a lesser woman, she would have quit the contract and not shown up for work. But she wasn't. And she wasn't a coward. If Petros even came near her, she had a few choice words for him.

But, much to her surprise, Petros kept his distance. She spied him in his office, working hard, his usual stony stare directed at his computer screen or to whomever was in front of him at the moment. He didn't glance her way when she walked by. To be absolutely sure, she even made several trips across the office.

Nope, he didn't look up or even break his concentration. Not even when she made sure to walk real slow. Just in case he didn't realize she was around.

Good. This was for the best. They should just ignore each other and pretend nothing happened. Like, nothing ever happened between them. Not that first kiss. Or the second one.

Ugh.

She shoved her headphones over her ears and turned to

her computer. But even as she tried to work, a small itch formed deep inside her. She ignored it, but it began to grow until she just couldn't get it out of her head.

Did she go too far yesterday? Okay, maybe tossing the bear to the ground, then at him, was a little dramatic. But the memories of Tommy made her do that.

Petros didn't know.

Of course he didn't know. That was a million years ago. She got out of that situation if a little scarred. And Tommy, that emotionally abusive asshole, had to leave town after she got her revenge.

She popped her head over the cubicle again. Petros wasn't in his office. Where did he go? Her mind immediately went to that skank, Agatha. Was she around here? The bitch sent dagger eyes at her whenever they ran into each other. It was obvious she wanted Petros for herself. Well, she could have him for all she cared.

"Kate?"

She nearly jumped out of her skin. Petros was standing right behind her. *Speak of the devil.* "What?" she snapped.

"Christina would like to see us in the conference room," he said, his voice all business-like.

"Give me one minute. I need to save my work and close out of the system."

He gave her a curt nod and left without saying anything else. She stared after him, dumbfounded for a moment. *Well,* a voice inside her said. *This is what you wanted, right?*

Right.

She saved her program and picked up her laptop, placing it under her arm. Entering the empty conference room, she sat on the first chair on the right. A minute passed, and she was still alone.

Since there was no one here, Kate opened the lid of her laptop and scrolled to the saved page on her web browser. *Yes!* She put in the initial bid for the Chevelle this morning and so far, no one had outbid her yet.

"Nice car," Christina said as she looked over Kate's shoulder. Petros walked in after her and took the seat opposite from Kate.

"Uh, thanks," she said, not bothering to hide the fact that she was dicking around on the web during office hours. They were the ones who called her to this meeting and arrived late.

"Chevelle, right? Nineteen Seventy?" Christina asked as she sat at the head of the table.

"Yeah. And she's gonna be all mine soon."

"Do you not own a car already? Something similar?" Petros asked.

Oh, so he was going to make small talk now? "That's Nathan's car. He's letting me borrow it while he's away."

His dark brows knitted together. "A car that is decades old doesn't seem like a good idea. Does it even have safety belts?"

Wow, the nerve of this Judgy McJudgerson. "If you must know, my dad and I are going to fix up the car, just as soon as he and Ma come back from their trip."

"Why did he not do it before?" he asked.

"Duh, because he worked on Nathan's first."

He scratched his head.

"What now?" she asked.

"Well, it seems strange to me that he would not restore your car of choice to ensure your safety before you left, yet he would gladly do it for his son."

"What?" Kate's voice rose. "You don't have any siblings, do you?"

Christina looked at Petros, then shot Kate a nervous look.

"It's not what you think," Kate continued. "See, while Nathan was, believe it or not, a good boy who got straight A's and loved spending time with our folks, I was the one who was always out, preferring to hang out with my ... friends." A lump in her throat began to form. "But as I got older, I realized how much my parents really cared about me. Besides, it's not like I can afford a car like that out of college. I'm saving up for it with my own cash."

Though her parents were comfortably wealthy, they never spoiled her or Nathan. Clark and Martha Caldwell taught their children the value of hard work. Nathan worked at the mines for four summers straight to buy his Mustang. Though Kate was still somewhat of a slacker, she worked for every single thing in her life.

"My apologies," Petros said in a tight voice.

"All right, children," Christina said, rolling her eyes. "Can we start?"

Kate gave Petros a dirty look then nodded at Christina.

The meeting took the better part of an hour, with Christina asking to make some changes to her software and Petros adding a few comments here and there. But for the most part, all the things they wanted were reasonable and would actually improve their workflow.

"Looks like everything is going smoothly," Christina said. "Thank you for your hard work, Kate." She gathered her things. "I need to go on a video call with my father in fifteen minutes, then Jason will want to leave as soon as I'm done so I best get on with my day."

They adjourned their meeting and closed up the conference room. As soon as they walked out the door, Agatha, who was all the way across the room, zeroed in on them, then began to walk their way.

"Petros," she said, her smile dazzling. "Are you finished with your meeting? There's something I need you to see."

"What is it?"

"It's …." Her gaze flickered over to Kate. "Classified. I can't just let *anyone* see this."

Her wolf wanted to smack this bitch up, and for once Kate wanted to give in. She wondered how much trouble she could get in, but with Christina right beside her, she guessed it would be *a lot*.

"Fine. Show me what it is." He nodded at Kate and Christina and followed Agatha to her cubicle.

"For what it's worth," Christina said, placing a reassuring hand on Kate's arm, "he's not interested. No matter what she's showing him."

"Ha!" She snorted. "I don't give a flying fuck."

"Uh-huh," Christina said. "Sure. I'll see you tomorrow."

Kate clenched her fists at her side, watching from afar as Petros went into Agatha's cubicle. When his head disappeared as he bent down, a burst of jealousy and rage made its way to the surface. She quickly turned away and stomped back to her desk.

Without a second thought, she grabbed her phone, scrolled through her contacts, and pressed the green "Call" button next to the name she had searched for.

"Hello?"

"Hey, it's me."

"Kate?" Amelia Walker's voice sounded surprised. "Hey, how've you been?"

She considered lying, but she had to take out the big guns to get what she wanted. "Not great." She sank down on the chair.

There was a pause. "What's wrong?"

"Amelia, I know you're coming back next week for Luke and Georgina's wedding, but ... could you come home this weekend too, please? I need you." She tried to sound desperate and sad so Amelia would give in, but there was no need. Kate was sure she sounded pathetic for real. "Let's have a girls' weekend."

"Of course," Amelia replied without hesitation. "What do you want to do? Drinking at The Den? Or we can go to my folks' place and you, me, and Sybil can gorge on junk food and watch horror movies all night?"

All those suggestions sounded nice. But maybe something different would do her some good. "Why don't we go to the lake? Your dad still has the cabin there, right? The one next to Uncle Hank and Aunt Riva's?"

"I'll grab the keys from Ben, and we can head over on Saturday morning."

She breathed a sigh of relief. "Thank you, Amelia."

"Anytime, hun. Do you want to chat for a bit? I have some time."

"No, I'll wait until Saturday. Thanks again."

"No prob. See you then."

Kate put the phone down. Amelia, along with Sybil, was one of her best friends. She was also the strongest out of all of them and was initially the one who helped her see how blind she was during the whole Tommy debacle. And yet, fierce as Amelia was, even she had her limits. Until now, Kate still wanted to cut off that *jerk's* balls for what he did to drive her away from them. The coward left town eventually, but Amelia said she just couldn't come back because of all the painful memories.

She calmed herself with a deep breath. *Just get through the week, and you'll be fine.* But when her damn super shifter hearing picked up the sound of Agatha's giggle, she nearly crushed her phone in her hands.

You can do this, she said, giving herself a pep talk. *Get through the week.*

"Ah, this is amazing." Kate breathed in the fresh mountain air as they stood in front of the Walker cabin on Blackstone Lake. "Don't you think so, Sybil?"

Sybil grimaced as she slapped a bug that landed on her arm. "Why couldn't we have had our sleepover at the castle? You know we have a huge TV screen in the family room, and Meg will make us chocolate chip cookies."

Because I needed to get as far away from Blackstone as possible, Kate thought but bit her lip instead. "What, you don't like roughing it?"

Sybil stuck her tongue out at Kate. "When have I ever been a fan of roughing it? Remember the hiking trip to the Rockies when we were twelve?"

"Or the summer camp my dad sent us to?" Amelia piped in as she took the large cooler from the back of her SUV.

Kate giggled. "Oh yeah. But this is hardly roughing it." She nodded to the small cabin. "We have beds and running water."

"Yeah, but no Wi-Fi," Sybil said, wagging a finger at Kate. "You sure you won't mind?"

"Puh-lease! I can last without the Internet for a whole weekend."

"Hey, when you two are done yammering," Amelia called out. "You wanna give me a hand?"

"Sorry!" Kate and Sybil said in unison as they began to take down their bags and other things from the car. Despite all their luggage – "Why the hell do you need three bottles of sunscreen, Sybil?" – the three shifters made quick work of unpacking the car.

"Finally!" Amelia plopped down on the couch and spread her arms and legs out. "I've been driving for hours! I need a—hey!"

Kate giggled as she landed on top of Amelia. Sybil came at them and then threw herself on top of the two girls.

"Ow! Get off me you two lunatics!" Amelia cried, though she chuckled when Sybil and Kate threw their arms around her. She pulled them in for a fierce hug.

"I love bear hugs!" Kate cried.

"You two are too much," Amelia laughed.

"Just like old times," Sybil said as she rolled away and landed beside Amelia.

"I miss this," Kate said wistfully.

"So," Amelia began, her tone turning serious. "Are you going to tell me why I came all the way here?"

"Because you love me?" Kate asked, hoping she wouldn't have to explain to Amelia or even have to think about the whole Petros thing.

Amelia raised a brow at her and gave her the "you-can't-hide-anything-from-me" look.

"Fine." Kate took a deep breath and caught up Amelia with the whole Petros situation.

"So," Amelia said when Kate finished. "A wolf from Lykos wants you to be his mate."

"Then he best go back there," Kate replied with a snort.

"Let me get this straight: at first, he went all Alpha male on you. You asked him to stop," Amelia continued, "and now he's treating you with respect and hasn't said anything about being mates?"

She shook her head.

"So what's the problem, then?" Amelia said. "You got what you wanted, right?"

"Right." *Maybe.* He really did fuck up with the gifts and she got tired of him pushing the whole mate thing in her face, but this treating her with cold indifference and acting like nothing had ever happened seemed worse somehow. Her wolf agreed and it had been a total bitch the whole week, whining and crying and then making her feel all jealous whenever Agatha or any other female got too close to Petros.

"Oh my God," Sybil said. "You want him."

"What?" she said in an incredulous voice. "I do not!"

"Yes, you do!" Sybil retorted. "*Baaaaaad.* Why else would you have your panties in a bunch right now?"

"*Do* you want him?" Amelia asked.

"Well, he's pretty hot," she admitted. Okay, more than hot. Like, melt her entire underwear drawer *hot.* "But this mate thing is too much! Why do I have to buy the whole pig to get a little sausage?"

Sybil lobbed a pillow at her head. "Kate, you're disgusting."

"What? It's true! Maybe I'm just horny since I haven't seen any action in a while." She grabbed her phone. "I should install that app—"

"Nuh-uh!" Sybil grabbed the phone and took it away. When Kate made a grab for it, she slipped it down her bra.

"Don't think she won't try to get in there," Amelia warned. "You know she's always envied your boobs."

"She can try, but you know it's in too deep." Sybil smirked with a nod to her generous cleavage. "I forbid you from hooking up with some random guy to try and get over Petros. He's your *mate*. Have some decency for once!"

"You're being an uptight —"

"I'm thinking of moving back home!" Amelia blurted out.

"What?" Both Kate and Sybil stopped and stared at her, their fight seemingly forgotten.

"Really?" Kate said, hope blooming in her chest.

"Yeah." Amelia gave them a sad smile. "After those guys tried to blow up Blackstone, I realized I can't stay away just because of what happened in the past. I mean, I could have lost everyone in that attack." Her eyes misted over as her voice broke. "I should have been here, helping. And with Ben and Penny having the baby, well, I'm going to be an aunt, and they'll need me, too."

"Oh Amelia!" Sybil threw her arms around her. "I'm so happy! This is great news!"

"Yay!" Kate jumped up. "Woot! Let's celebrate!" She whipped off her shirt, revealing her bikini top. "Last one in the lake's a rotten egg!"

"No fair!" Sybil cried. "I don't have my suit on!"

"You don't need a suit, dearie!" Kate said. "Just go out the way nature intended you to!" She didn't wait for Sybil's retort as she raced out of the cabin and down the dock that ran over the lake. She let out a loud cry and jumped into the water.

The lake was cold but refreshing, and she paddled around a bit and moved to the shallow part. A few seconds later, Amelia and Sybil came out, wearing their swimsuits, and jumped in beside her, splashing water all over Kate.

"Gahh!" Kate wiped her face. "You morons!" She splashed them and they retaliated, which turned into a full-on water splashing war.

The sound of car engines made them freeze. Kate's wolf raised its hackles, and her two friends' faces changed, all of them on alert. No one else lived in Blackstone Lake, as it was private property, owned by the Lennoxes. Who could it be?

"Hey, when you girls are done dicking around, you should come over!"

All three of them looked toward the sound of the voice. Jason Lennox was standing in the water a few feet from them, parallel to right about where Uncle Hank's cabin was located beside Uncle James'.

Sybil waved to her brother. "I didn't know you guys were planning to be here!"

Jason scowled. "It's not a romantic weekend getaway, if that's what you're thinking." He waded over to them.

"Where's Christina?" Amelia asked. "And what do you mean it's not a romantic getaway?"

The dragon shifter jerked his thumb behind him. "Christina thought this would be a good time to bring her team over for some R and R. They'd been working hard and everything, so they're here as a reward."

Sybil nudged Amelia. "That's him. Petros. Kate's ma—"

"Shut your dirty mouth!" Kate said, splashing water at Sybil and Amelia.

"Hey!" Amelia sputtered, spitting out the lake water. "What the—oh wow."

She followed Amelia's gaze toward the Lennox side of the shore. There was a group there already, but her eyes were immediately drawn to Petros. He was wearing a pair of very brief swimming trunks and carried two coolers over his shoulder. When he bent over to set them down, Kate couldn't stop herself from groaning softly.

"Kate, that is Grade A sausage meat," Amelia stage-whispered.

Had it been anyone else, Kate's wolf would have scratched Amelia's eyes out. But her wolf knew Amelia was a friend.

However, when she saw the figure sauntering over to Petros, she immediately felt her claws come out.

"Oh God. Could she possibly wear any less clothing without being completely naked?" Sybil snorted.

Agatha was indeed wearing one of the skimpiest bikinis Kate had ever seen, if you could even call it that. The scraps of lycra covered her nipples and the important bits, but as Agatha turned around, it was obvious those were the only parts they covered.

"Wow, I'm glad I'm not a wolf shifter," Amelia drolled. "Or I'd be howling at the moon."

Kate said nothing, though when Agatha moved closer to Petros and put a hand on his bicep, she couldn't watch anymore and turned away.

"Come over for a beer," Jason said. "We have lots."

"We came prepared, too," Amelia laughed. "But I would like to catch up with Christina for a bit."

"I'm going for a swim," Kate declared. "You guys go on ahead."

"Kate—"

"I'll be fine, Amelia." She turned away, slunk down, and paddled away from them.

When she was far enough away, she let out a frustrated cry. Was it really a coincidence that *he* was here at the same time she was having a girl's weekend? It could well have been, but she had a feeling it wasn't. *Damn Christina and her meddling.* Why couldn't she just mind her own business?

"Who cares?" she said to no one in particular. She wasn't going to let anyone ruin her fun. She was going to have the best time ever, and Amelia moving back to Blackstone was icing on the cake. She had to see the bright side of things.

Kate waded back to their cabin and pulled herself up on

the dock, then laid out on the wooden platform, letting the sun warm her chilled body. She wasn't sure how long she was lying there, but she huffed unhappily as she heard the sounds of laughter, chatter, and music from the other side of the privacy shrubbery installed between the two cabins. Where were Sybil and Amelia? This was supposed to be a weekend for the three of them.

With an unhappy grunt, she lowered herself back into the water to paddle over to the Lennox side. The team from The Agency was nowhere to be seen, though she spotted Amelia and Sybil chatting with Jason and Christina, seemingly oblivious to Kate's presence.

An idea struck her. Kate had to bite her lip to stop the evil laugh from escaping her mouth. Oh, this would surely bring back the memories from that disastrous summer camp. They would all have a good laugh about it afterward.

She waded out deeper into the water, and when she was satisfied, she began to flail her arms. "Sybil! Amelia!" she called out as her head dipped up and down the water line. "Help! I'm cramping."

Secretly, she was snickering inside. As soon as her friends came, she would pull them down under the water. When she did this all those years ago, she had accidentally yanked Sybil's bikini top off. The dragon shifter had been so mad at her when she flashed the junior counselor, she didn't speak to Kate for a week. But it had been worth it to see Sybil's face, and they made up for it later when Kate brought her a box of pastries from Rosie's.

"Sybil!" she cried. Where the fuck were her friends? "Amelia!" Didn't they care about her? She heard a loud splash coming from their direction. *Finally!*

Kate twisted around, trying to make a grab for a limb or a

leg, but her hand hit a solid wall. No, not a wall. It was someone's chest.

"Mother—" The wind knocked out of her as a strong arm pulled her up from the water. *Not again!* She didn't bother struggling and went limp instead. It would be no use anyway. But maybe she could have some fun.

Petros's grip around her was like steel, and Kate could feel his body tense as they walked up to the shore by the Walker cabin. He dropped to his knees and gently laid her on the sand. She kept her eyes closed and held her breath.

"Kate!" he said, placing his ear near her mouth. "Please, say something."

Kate grinned and then spit the water she had been holding in her mouth against his cheek.

Petros wiped his face and then looked down at her and blinked. "You are unhurt?"

"I'm fine, you big lug!" she hissed. "I wasn't drowning for real."

The expression on his face changed, like the sudden arrival of a storm on a bright day. His mouth twisted in anger, and his eyes turned dark. "You think drowning is funny?" His voice was terse and cutting.

"It was a *joke*," she said, rolling her eyes. "A bit of fun."

"I thought you were in danger! That you were dy—" He growled. "You will not do that again!"

What the fuck was his problem? "Oh yeah? Who's gonna make me?"

The words came out of her mouth much faster than she'd anticipated, and now she wished she'd chosen her words more carefully. Or said them another time, like when she wasn't underneath him.

"You are a brat," he spat. He grabbed her wrists and pinned them over her head with one hand.

"And you're an asshole who doesn't have a funny bone in his body!" Damn her mouth!

Petros' eyes went crazy, and Kate braced herself for what was coming. She knew he wouldn't hurt her, but the look in his eyes ... it was like she could see the demons he held tightly reigned along with his wolf. She could also sense that control about to break, like an overflowing dam.

His lips were savage as they came down on hers. She should have struggled more instead of kissing him back. She should have pushed him away instead of spreading her thighs so he could press his hips against her. *Oh fucking hell*. With those tiny Speedos, he might as well have worn nothing. Her pussy flooded with her wetness, and she pushed her hips seeking the friction that made her shiver.

Kate moaned when he moved his lips lower, whimpering at the loss of his mouth on hers. He licked his wicked tongue down the column of her neck, his lips sucking at the sensitive spots on her skin. She dug her fingers into his hair, pulling him down toward her breasts. Petros yanked the top of her bikini down and immediately popped a nipple into his mouth.

The heat and wetness made her moan, and if that wasn't enough, Petros' hand moved lower. He lifted his hips from hers as his eager fingers moved under her bikini bottoms. She was already soaking wet, but she was gushing now as his digits pressed against her pussy lips. Damn, between his mouth and fingers, she was like one giant hormone.

"Petros," she cried as his fingers dipped inside her, and his mouth sucked her nipple deeper. "Oh God! Fucking hell!" She scratched her nails down his back as she thrust her hips up to meet his fingers. His thumb found her clit and the moment he plucked the bud, her body shook with a powerful orgasm.

Hot damn. Her vision went white briefly, and she wasn't sure if it was from coming or from staring up at the sun. When it returned to normal, she found herself looking up at ocean-colored eyes. Petros' gaze was intense but not angry anymore. Instead, she could feel the desire radiating from them.

"Let's go inside," she breathed. "Please." She needed him bad. On top of her. Inside her.

He nodded and got to his feet, picking her up. She clung to him as he carried her inside. Amelia was going to be pissed if she had sex in her parents' cabin, but Kate could deal with that later. Right now, she just needed Petros.

Petros pushed the door open and planted her on the nearest surface—the kitchen counter. Not what she was thinking of, but then she couldn't really imagine having sex in the bed in the loft upstairs, considering this was Uncle James' cabin. She spread her knees and grabbed his bicep, then pulled him close.

His mouth captured hers again, and she moved her hands down to slip under his trunks. She dug her nails into his firm ass, which made him groan.

"I've dreamed of this for so long, Kate-mine," he whispered in her ear. "To give you pleasure and to make you my mate. You will be truly mine."

Kate felt like someone doused her with a bucket of cold water. She took her hands out of his trunks and pushed him away. "Petros, you know this is just sex, right?"

"You are—what?"

She swallowed audibly. "I mean, this. We're two horny adults. It doesn't have to mean anything." No, she couldn't be anyone's. She vowed to herself that she would never belong to someone who would control her ever again.

"You think this is just about sex?" he said, stepping away from her.

He was angry again. She could feel it radiating off him in waves. Well, she was furious, too. She hopped off the counter and pushed at him. "What you want from me, Petros, I can't give." She just couldn't. Not again.

"Why do you deny yourself?" he asked.

"I thought that was what this was about? To stop denying ourselves?" He was making this so difficult! "Why the hell did you jump in the water anyway?"

"To save you! I thought you were drowning!"

"Well, you should have let me die then!"

Petros' eyes glowed with a dangerous light. The power, anger, and loathing that radiated from him made Kate stagger back. He let out a pained roar, turned on his heel, and walked out the door. The sound of the door slamming made Kate grab the counter in fright.

She stood there, feeling the adrenaline leave her system, shock taking its place. What the hell just happened? She thought they were having fun. Clearly, he had misunderstood her intentions.

"That asshole!" She brought down a fist on the counter. He was the one sending mixed signals. Ignoring her and then letting that skank Agatha rub her tits all over him the whole week. Then jumping in to "save" her like he was some hero. He kissed *her* first!

"Kate? What are you ... oh my God!" Amelia exclaimed, taking a deep breath. "Did you have sex in here?"

"No!" she denied. "I mean ...." She bit her lip.

"What's going on?" Sybil said, coming up from behind Amelia.

"Apparently, Kate did *not* have sex on my parents' kitchen counter," Amelia said, rolling her eyes.

"You had sex with Petros?" Sybil asked, confused.

"What? I said I didn't!" Kate protested. "Well, almost, but ... ugh!" She walked over to the fridge and grabbed the bottle of wine chilling on the shelf. "Can we just get on with our girls' weekend please?" She unscrewed the top and took a healthy swig. It was going to take a hell of a lot of alcohol to get her drunk, and even more to make her forget about Petros, but it was a good thing she was prepared.

CHAPTER SEVEN

"Fun weekend?" Christina asked as Kate entered her office.

Kate plopped down on the chair in front of the other woman's desk and lowered her dark glasses down to the bridge of her nose. "Yeah, it was. But don't worry; this hangover'll be gone in an hour or two."

"How much did you have to drink?" Christina asked.

"Not enough." Kate pulled the glasses over her eyes again. "So, that's one dirty move you pulled."

"Excuse me?"

"Having your fun little team building exercise the same weekend I'm having my girls' night with my best friends?" she accused. *Ouch.* Even the sound of her own voice made her head throb. She probably shouldn't have had that tequila this morning, but she vowed to drink every last bottle of liquor they had brought for the trip, and she was no quitter.

Christina stood up and walked over to her side of the table. "Kate," she said as she sat down on the chair opposite from her, "Did something happen between you and Petros?"

"Ha! I wish something did! Then at least I'd have gotten a

good screwing out of this mess. God, I hate men!" She shot to her feet. "Tell me, are all guys from Lykos stubborn, confusing, and infuriating assholes?"

Christina's brows furrowed together. "Why don't we talk about it?"

"Talk about what?" Kate whipped the glasses off her face. "How that stupid man kept going on and on about being mates, and then he ignores me for a week? How he says I'm his mate, and we're going to be together, and then lets that *bitch* sniff around him? Or how he saves me when I'm pretending to be drowning and—"

"Hold on!" Christina raised a hand. "You what?"

"I was playing this trick I did with Sybil and Amelia when we were at this God-awful camp one summer," Kate explained. "I went into the water and started flailing my arms, pretending I was drowning. They were supposed to jump in—"

"No!" Christina gripped Kate's arms. "You didn't!"

"I did."

"*Gamisou!*" Christina's face faltered. "Sit down, Kate."

"I don't—"

"Sit. *Down.*"

Christina's face had gone completely serious, and Kate didn't have a choice but to plant her butt on the seat. For a human, Christina sure was scary. "Okay," she said. "Now what?"

"Has Petros ever talked about his past? What happened when he was a child?"

Kate shook her head.

"Or about any recent events?"

"No."

Christina paced back and forth. "I swear, I'm going to lock

you two in a room until you sort this out! No wonder Petros has been on a tear since Saturday!"

"Wait, what's going on?" Kate asked.

With a long sigh, Christina sat down. "This isn't some big secret, so I'll tell you. Petros wasn't one of us. I mean, he wasn't born on Lykos."

"He wasn't?"

"No. Petros washed up on one of the beaches on the island when he was a young boy, maybe four or five. An old fisherman and his wife found him. They thought he was dead, but they were able to revive him."

Kate gasped. "What happened to him?"

"We don't know exactly," Christina said. "But a few days later, they found two more bodies. A man and a woman. His parents, most likely. Petros was too young to remember anything, but we think they were trying to seek sanctuary in Lykos. There was a storm, and their boat must have capsized."

"Oh no." Dread filled her as she thought of Petros as a young boy in a boat with his parents. How scared he must have been. And his poor parents ….

"We took him in, of course. He was a wolf, after all. The fisherman and his wife raised him," Christina explained.

"His biological parents … drowned?"

"Yes," Christina said.

Oh. My. God. Then she realized something. "*I'm* the asshole," Kate exclaimed and covered her hands with her face. Petros saw her drowning and probably relived the trauma of losing his mother and father.

"That's not all," Christina said.

"There's more?"

She nodded. "A few months ago, there was a mission in Cyprus. The Agency traced sources of bloodsbane being manufactured somewhere on an island off the coast. Petros went in with his team, but they were expecting them. Looking back now, they were probably part of The Organization. His team was ambushed."

Kate swallowed the lump in her throat. "Did they make it out?"

"Most of them did," Christina said. "Except for one. Milos, his best friend growing up. They were making their escape on a boat, but Milos was shot and tumbled overboard."

"Oh no." Kate really felt like dirt now. No wait. Was there something lower than dirt?

Christina gave her a weak smile. "You didn't know. But that doesn't excuse all this bad behavior. From either of you," she clarified. "You guys need to talk. I know I've been a bit pushy, but you know … Petros, he's a great guy. He's saved my ass a couple of times in the field. You couldn't ask for a better mate."

"I …" She wasn't sure about the mate part, but Kate knew when she was in the wrong. "I'll apologize right away." She stood up.

"Umm, give him some time, okay?" Christina said. "And if he doesn't accept your apology, don't give up easily. You guys are mates; it'll all work out."

The words made her chest constrict, but she found every ounce of confidence she had, balled it together, and held onto it. "Thank you, Christina."

"I have faith in you."

Kate nodded. She needed every bit of help she could.

Kate went straight to her cubicle, trying not to look over at

Petros' office as she walked by. He probably wouldn't even glance her way, anyway. As she sat down and opened her laptop, she tried to work but couldn't concentrate. For one thing, her wolf was furious at her, scratching and growling at her. How could she hurt their mate like that?

I don't know. I'm just a great big jerk, I guess.

She wanted to wait and figure out what to do, but she couldn't sit still and just do nothing. The image of Petros as a kid, losing his parents and then later his best friend, kept popping up in her mind. The urge to make things right was much too strong, and she got up and marched over to his office. Her heart hammered, but she kept on until she reached the door. She saw Petros inside through the glass and didn't bother to knock as she opened the door.

"Petros, I—"

But he wasn't alone. *Fuckity fuck fuck fuck!* Of course *she* had to be here. Agatha turned her head toward her with an eyebrow raised.

"Don't you know how to knock?" he asked, irritation in his voice.

Agatha said nothing, but her red-painted lips curled into a smile.

"I—I need to talk to you."

"Then speak," he said. He was looking at her, but at the same time, he wasn't. It was like she wasn't there, and his gaze was passing through her.

"In private."

"You can say what you need to now or wait and make an appointment."

"I just ..." *Just say it!* "I'll wait. Later."

Dejected, she turned around with her head hung low as she walked back to her cubicle. She swore she felt Agatha's sneer, even with her back turned. Someday, she was going to get back at that bitch, but for now, she had to figure out how to make Petros listen to her, if not forgive her.

She bided her time, waiting until six p.m. when most of the staff were shutting down their computers and getting ready to leave. Petros was also packing up, and she quickly ran out of the office. Skipping the elevator, she went to the staircase, taking the steps two at a time so she could get to the parking lot faster. She spied Petros' truck where he usually parked it, strode over, and waited.

She didn't have to wait too long as she immediately saw him as he exited the glass doors of Lennox Corp. He seemed distracted and didn't notice her until he was a few feet away.

Blue-green eyes turned to steel. "What are you doing here?"

"I told you I'd wait for later."

"For what?"

"So we can talk."

"About what?"

Stubborn wolf! "I wanted to say sorry. For ... everything."

He didn't move a muscle, but she saw a tick in his jaw. "You'll need to be more specific than that."

"I—"

"Petros! Petros!" came the breathy voice from behind. "Sorry, I did have my keys in my purse." Agatha's gaze turned to Kate, her eyes sharp and cold. "What is *she* doing here?"

"What am I doing here?" She clenched her fists at her side. The growl was in her throat, but she swallowed it. *No*, she told her wolf. Don't give her the satisfaction. "Are you headed somewhere?"

"There's this new bar in town, Argo's," she said. "We're headed there for a drink."

"All of us," Petros added, waving to a group of agents who were walking in the parking lot. "Agatha is riding with me, so we all don't have to drive."

"We just had so much fun over the weekend and wanted to hang out again. We would have invited you," Agatha said in a sickly sweet voice, "but we didn't want you to feel left out since you're not one of us."

Petros shot Agatha a warning look. "It's not—"

"It's fine," Kate said, pasting a smile on her face. "I heard about that new place. It's some big corporate chain, right? I don't know; I think The Den is still way cooler."

"Maybe it's time Blackstone had some competition," Agatha said. "Something shiny and new."

"Well, people might be dazzled by shiny new things, but there's nothing like a classic." She bit her tongue. "Have a nice night."

Kate pivoted on her heel, not bothering to wait for another cutting remark from that skank. She'd been humiliated enough, after all, and she knew when it was time to back down.

Petros didn't want her apology. No, wait; he didn't want *her*. And it was all her own damn fault.

CHAPTER EIGHT

Kate wanted to drown her sorrows, and she knew the perfect place to do it.

As Rosie put the chocolate peanut butter pie with extra-extra whipped cream on the table, the fox shifter asked, "Did you need some plates?"

She looked up at Rosie glumly. "Just a fork will do."

Rosie shrugged and placed a fork on the table, gave her a reassuring squeeze on the shoulder, then walked away.

Kate stabbed the pie with her fork and shoved a big piece in her mouth. The chocolate and peanut butter concoction was amazing, and she felt somewhat satisfied. She was halfway done with the pie when someone slipped into the seat in front of her.

"What's wrong *now*?" Sybil asked. "You said you were fine when we dropped you off last night."

"Nothing's wrong," Kate said as she swallowed another forkful of pie. She licked the steel clean, dug it into the tin, and offered Sybil a bite. "Want some?"

The dragon shifter grimaced. "No, that's unsanitary."

"We drank from the same six bottles of vodka over the weekend, and *this* is unsanitary?" Kate said. "Well, more for me then."

Sybil reached over and gripped her wrists, making Kate drop the fork. "Who are you and what have you done to my best friend?"

"Excuse me? What are you doing here, anyway?"

Sybil released her. "Rosie called me," she said and cocked her head toward the fox shifter. Rosie looked back at them and flashed them a knowing smile. "She said you weren't looking like yourself, and I needed to come down and rescue you."

Kate stared down at the half-eaten dish. "From her pies?"

"From yourself!" Sybil said in an exasperated voice. "Now, tell me what happened."

Kate took a long, deep breath, then told Sybil what had transpired that day. "... And now he won't even look at me. I'm just ... I think I've really done it this time, Sybil. I don't know if he'll forgive me."

"Kate," Sybil began. "What you did was pretty bad, but it's not unforgivable. You didn't know what happened to him when he was a kid."

"Then why is he so mad at me?"

"Have you considered it's not just that one incident? Sure, Petros hasn't exactly been a gentleman, and he can be stubborn. But all he wants is *you*. He doesn't care about who you are or what happened to you before."

"It's the mating bond," Kate pointed out.

"And so what if it is?" Sybil countered. "It just means fate or whatever or whoever out there in the universe thinks you guys are perfect for each other. Why are you fighting it? Is it because of that jerk, Tommy? It's been years, Kate; are you still going to let him have control over you after all this time?"

The words made her freeze.

Oh God.

Sybil was right. All this time she thought she was free of Tommy, but she was avoiding relationships because of him. Somehow, even though he was gone from her life, he was still controlling her. Her aversion to Petros calling her "mine" was a reflex on her part, but her wolf knew he wasn't like Tommy.

"He won't even talk to me. This is it. I've made a mess of things, and there's no way I can fix it."

Sybil brought her palms down on the table, sending the pie tin clattering across the surface. "Stop thinking like that!"

The smoke curling out of Sybil's nose made Kate nearly jump out of her seat. "Sybil?"

"You're Kate *motherfucking* Caldwell! You're going to *make* him listen." She stood up, pushing the chair behind her a few feet and sending it crashing to the wall. "Oops! Sorry, Rosie!" She gave the proprietress a sheepish smile. "I'll pay for that." Sybil turned back to Kate. "C'mon."

"Wait, where are we going?"

Sybil was already tugging Kate toward the door. "We're going to Argo's!"

"You're coming with me?" Kate asked.

"Of course," Sybil said. "If that skanky-ass ho comes near you, she's going to learn what dragon fire tastes like. I'm your ride-or-die-chick, don't you know?"

Kate laughed until tears sprang in her eyes. "I love you, Sybil."

"And I love you, you crazy chick! Now, let's go."

Argo's was located in South Blackstone, a newer part of town that Lennox Corp. was developing to attract a younger demographic to live and work in the town. It was all industrial and modern, and several condos, as well as bars, shops, and restaurants had popped up over the last couple of years. Nathan's loft was actually not far from where they were.

"What the fuck is this place?" Kate exclaimed as they entered the door.

"Are we supposed to be in space or something?" Sybil asked.

Argo's had that ultra-cool industrial look inside, with sleek glass decor, black metal countertops, and stainless steel furniture. The waitresses were dressed in super tight silver dresses and carried trays of fancy cocktails. Some kind of modern "song" that sounded like an out of tune harpsichord and a timpani had a mutant child was playing over the speaker.

"Ugh. I can't believe they let this place open in Blackstone," Sybil said.

"The price of progress, I suppose," Kate said. "It doesn't matter, anyway." Hopefully, they wouldn't be staying too long.

"Where is he?" Sybil asked.

Kate looked around. "There."

The Agency team was gathered around several tables, and they were all chatting and laughing, seemingly having a good time. Kate's gaze immediately landed on Petros, who was standing near the bar all by himself.

"Go," Sybil urged.

But Kate's feet were frozen. On the drive here she had been confident, finally realizing what had been holding her back all this time. Seeing him, however, was an entirely different story, and the air squeezed out of her lungs so hard it hurt. Thinking about how he looked at her today—with those cold, dead eyes—made her feel like her chest was caving in. She would rather he was angry at her, like he had been that day at the lake, instead of the cold indifference he was showing.

"He's leaving!" Sybil said. Petros had put down a few bills on the bar and was heading toward the side exit. "Go after him!"

"I—Shit!" Kate spotted Agatha looking around the bar. Her eyes narrowed as they landed on Petros' retreating back, and she grabbed her purse.

"Is that her?" Sybil asked.

"Yeah." Kate was seeing red. "How much cash do you have on you?"

"Why?"

Kate growled. "I'll need bail money because they're gonna put me in jail after I check a bitch!"

"No need." Sybil rolled up her shirt sleeves. "I'll take care of her."

"Okay ... wait, are you really going to set her on fire?"

Sybil choked. "What? No! I'll improvise. You go after Petros, and I'll make sure you guys aren't disturbed."

"Thanks, Sybil. You're the best." Kate sprinted to where Petros was headed, getting in front of Agatha. She heard a loud crash behind her and an indignant shriek, and she gave another silent thanks to her best friend.

Pushing against the exit door, she left the building and glanced around. The lot was half-empty, so it was easy to spot Petros as he strode to his parked truck.

Now or never.

Kate ran toward him. "Petros!"

He froze, his hand still on the door of his truck. Slowly, he turned around, then crossed his arms over his chest when he saw her. "What do you want?"

She swallowed, hoping it would clear the tight burning in her throat. "Petros, please I—"

"You've already said what you needed to say." His jaw was tight and his eyes like hard glass. He was doing it again. Looking through her like she wasn't there.

She ignored the stabbing pain in her chest. "I want to apologize. For my behavior for the past weeks. You're right; I am a brat." For a moment she thought she saw a crack in his expression, so she continued. "Christina told me."

"She told you what?"

"Everything. About you. Your parents and your best friend—"

Petros roared and slammed his hand on the hood of the truck. "She had no right!"

"She told me so I could understand why you acted that way at the lake. And I realize I was an asshole, pretending to— to do that."

Pain crossed his face. "I didn't want you to know that way. I never wanted you to know at all."

"Why not?" Her stomach clenched, and it was like she could feel his pain, too. "Why would you keep that from me?"

"So you wouldn't have to know how broken I am!" He took a step toward her. His wolf was on the edge now, snapping and biting, but she wasn't scared. "If you did, then you would never accept the mating bond! Why would you?"

"Petros ..." She placed a hand on his chest, his heart beating wildly against her palm. "Why would you think any of that would matter to me?"

He stared down at her. "When I washed up on the shores of Lykos, I had nothing," he began. "The couple who adopted me, they did it out of obligation. Because the Alpha told them to. They weren't unkind, but they treated me like a chore. A burden. The old man died when I was twenty years old, and I took care of the wife out of duty until she passed. Now that they were both gone, I feel nothing except some passing sadness."

The gasp escaped from her lips involuntarily, and she had to cover her mouth to stop from sobbing.

"Though my home life was not ideal, I grew up around the other children in Lykos. One of them was Milos." He paused. "He became my best friend. His mother treated me like her own son, gave me affection when I had none at home." His lips set into a tight line. "I was the one who told her about her son's death and held her in my arms as she broke down in her kitchen."

"Oh. God." Kate could feel the tears streaming down her cheeks. "Petros, it wasn't your fault."

"But it was," he said. "He was shot and fell overboard. We didn't notice until it was too late. If he didn't die of his injuries, then surely the sea took him. I was the team leader. His friend. I should have been standing at the back of the boat to check if we were being followed and—"

"No!" Kate threw herself at him, wrapping her arms around his waist and pressing her face to his chest. "No, no, no! Don't say that." The thought of him dying ... it was driving her and her wolf crazy.

She felt a hand rubbing down her back in a soothing manner. "Kate, there is nothing for me to forgive. I was the one who acted out of line that day. You didn't know all of this. The demons of my past took over. When I saw you in the water, I reacted."

Kate pulled away and looked up at him. "Petros, it's not

just about that day. This whole time ... I've been letting my past demons control me too, punishing you for something that's not your fault."

He tensed. "Your former boyfriend?"

"How—"

"Sybil mentioned him but did not go into detail. But I gathered enough to know he hurt you deeply."

Kate's breath hitched. "He did. But it wasn't just me. Because of what he did, I ignored my friends and family. Pushed everyone away, even my parents. He hurt all of them, too. And finally, after Amelia and Sybil were able to knock some sense into me, I told myself I would never let anyone control me like that again. That I would never let anyone own me."

His arms loosened around her. "Then you must forgive me."

"Huh?"

"For presuming that just because we are mates you would immediately fall into my arms. Or making it seem like I owned you."

"I was so shocked," she said. "I didn't think I would ever find a mate. My parents weren't mates, you know, and they're perfectly happy together."

"I left Lykos because I knew my mate wasn't there," Petros explained. "I felt incredibly lucky to have found you so quickly. I just wanted someone to cherish forever. Someone I could make a home with, together."

"I don't know if I'm ready for all this," Kate confessed. "It's all going too fast." Her heart was beating a mile a minute, and the blood was rushing to her brain so quickly she felt like she was going to faint. But, being in Petros' arms, inhaling his fresh ocean scent, it all felt right. Still, her natural, human instinct was to fight it with all her might.

"Then we can take it slow," he said. "I will not rush you anymore, Kate-m—" He stopped himself before he continued.

"No—I mean, you can still call me that." Oh God, was she blushing? *Grrr* ... Kate *motherfucking* Caldwell did not blush!

"You like it when I call you Kate-mine?"

"I ... it's growing on me," she said, but pressed her cheek to his chest to hide her face. As she breathed his scent in again, she felt him relax.

"Go out with me. On a date," he said. "Please."

"Are you asking me out?" she asked, raising a brow at him.

He grinned at her. "Yes. Yes, I am. Should I get down on one knee?"

"Don't you dare—hey!" She slapped him playfully. "You're messing with me, aren't you?"

"And you said I didn't have a single funny bone."

"Why you—Hmm .... " Oh, those lips again. She sank against him, enjoying the feel of his arms around her and being pressed up to his warm, hard body as his mouth moved over hers in a kiss. This was soft and slow and really very sweet, but it still sent tingles over her skin.

"I just had to," he said when he pulled away. "It's been too long since I've tasted you."

"It's only been two days." God, he was so intense. But she had to admit, she liked it.

"Like I said, too long." He let go of her and stepped back. "I want to do this the right way. To court you properly."

"Court me?" Okay, while that seemed corny, she couldn't help but find it sweet.

"Yes. I will take you to a nice dinner. We will have conversations and get to know each other," he said.

Oooh, that sounded nice.

"Perhaps we can take a nice stroll somewhere."

Hmm, romantic, but she wanted to know about the main event. "And then afterward …?"

"Afterward, I will take you home …"

"Yes?" *Oh God, please say you want to fuck my brains out!*

"And say goodnight."

"What?" she asked, her voice raising.

"Then we will go out again the following day."

She pouted. "That's it?"

He laughed. "Kate-mine, while your delectable body is tempting, I also want you to get to know me before we become intimate." He lowered his voice. "Because when we make love, there will be no going back."

Kate shivered. "I already—"

The loud sound of a door slamming open and hitting the wall made them pull apart. "Sybil?"

Sybil walked briskly toward them, her eyes darting around her. There was a red stain down the front of her white blouse, and her hair was all wet. "Kate! Are you done? We gotta go!"

"Go?" Kate asked, confused. "Why?"

"I … er … took care of … that thing … oh, hi Petros!" she greeted.

"What the hell happened?" Kate asked.

"Well, I kind of … set fire to Agatha's hair."

"You what?"

"It was an accident! And she was being a bitch!" Sybil said. "I stopped her from … you know … by running into her. Unfortunately, she was holding a glass of wine." She motioned to the front of her blouse. "It spilled over both of us. So then she started shouting at me in Greek. I offered to help clean up, but when we went to the bathroom, I lent her my sweater while I was washing out her blouse. She was standing over me, berating me the whole time, and I kind of 'accidentally' broke the tap and it sprayed all over her."

Kate had to bite her lip from giggling. "And then what happened?"

"So she gets even more mad at me, and she starts insulting me in English and calling me names," Sybil continued. "Her coworkers came in, and half of them were holding her back and the other half were threatening me. They were cornering me, and Agatha broke free of their grasp and ... it was a reflex, I swear!" she huffed, a puff of smoke escaping her nostrils. "I only singed her bangs."

"It's probably an improvement," Kate drolled.

"Anyway, can we get out of here, please?" Sybil begged. "I barely escaped."

Kate wanted to remind her she could turn into a twenty-foot fire-breathing dragon but held back. Besides, it's not like she was getting any action tonight, so she might as well go home and get some sleep. She glanced over at Petros. "I drove over, so I should take Sybil back to her car."

"Of course," he said with a nod. "But be ready after work?"

Oh, right. "I will." Damn, if Sybil weren't here, she could have maybe gotten to second base. Kate shot Petros an apologetic look, and he nodded at her.

"See you later, Petros!" Sybil said as she started dragging Kate away. "C'mon! I think I hear them coming!"

Kate groaned. "Fine, let's get out of here." She and Sybil would probably never come back to Argo's again but that wasn't going to be a problem. She'd stick to The Den from now on.

CHAPTER NINE

Petros watched the clock carefully. Was it broken? It seemed like more than a minute had passed since he last checked. Six o'clock couldn't seem to come fast enough.

He still couldn't believe what had happened last night. Kate had come to *him*. Her actions had hurt him deeply, and he had to admit he had lashed out at everyone around him after he left her in the cabin. He saw he was testing even Christina and Jason's patience, and he ended up leaving the lake earlier than the rest of the team who had stayed on until evening.

He was sullen and angry the whole weekend. He even let his wolf side take over, exploring the woods of the Blackstone Mountain and letting his animal take control. Anything to escape the pain of his mate's words and actions.

That was all in the past now. He had made mistakes; they both did. But now was the time to rectify them. That's why they had to start fresh. No matter how much he wanted to make love to her and claim her, he knew they had to take it slow. Sex was easy; it was everything else that was complicated. But all the misunderstandings would be behind them now.

"Finally," he muttered when, upon what seemed like his hundredth glance, the clock read one minute before six. *Close enough*, he thought as he shut down his computer and walked over to Kate's cubicle. It was difficult, trying not to get too close to her today, but he knew the anticipation only made it worth it.

When he reached her cubicle, he frowned when he didn't see any sign of her. Her jacket was not hanging off the back of the chair, and her desk was empty. There was a piece of paper on top with his name scrawled over the surface.

Meet you downstairs, it read when he turned it over. It was unsigned, but who else would it be from?

Petros checked in with the overnight crew and made his way to the lobby of the Lennox Corp. Building. He immediately spotted her by the doors, and when he saw what she was wearing, let out a soft groan.

Kate had probably left earlier to change because she definitely was not wearing *that* when she came into the office this morning. The short, tight black dress showed off her lithe figure and long legs, while the spiked heels emphasized her delicate ankles and calves. Her hair hung down her shoulders, and he noticed she had switched out the piercing in her nose from a clear jewel to one that was blue-green. Her lips were painted red, and she flashed him a wicked smile as he approached.

"This," he said, lowering his voice. "Is not fair."

"Oh?" she said. "Who said I played fair?"

He snorted. She wasn't making this easy, but then again, he didn't expect her to. "I've made reservations at Pistache French Bistro," he said. "Should we drive out separately?"

"Why don't we take my car?" she said. "You've never ridden in a Mustang, have you?"

"I have not had the pleasure," he said. He would have preferred to drive since he invited her out, but they didn't plan the logistics well enough. Two cars seemed unnecessary, and a single vehicle was more practical. "All right. Let's go."

Kate led him to where the bright yellow vehicle was parked and unlocked the door. He got into the passenger side seat. "It's very nice."

"The interior's all new," Kate said. "Luxury leather seats. Only the best for my brother."

As soon as he was settled, Kate flung her body across his. He startled, her delicious scent filling his nose as her soft body pressed against his. "Kate," he warned, though he couldn't stop himself from enjoying the feel of her.

She reached over, grabbed the seatbelt from over his right shoulder and pulled it across his body. "What?" she asked as the belt buckle clicked into place. "I just wanted to show you this car was safe." She gave him a sweet smile as she put her own belt on and slipped the key into the ignition.

Oh no, Kate definitely did *not* play fair.

"Do you know the way?" he asked as they made their way out of the parking lot.

"I haven't been there, but it's near the Ritz Ski Resort, right?"

He nodded. "It's a bit far out, but with everything in town mostly closed, I thought it would be the better choice."

"No prob," she said. "We'll get there in no time."

The engine revved a loud sound that made the car vibrate. Kate stepped on the pedal, and they sped down the highway.

"How's that for a classic American car?" she asked, her lips curling up. He didn't miss her breath hitch or the way her thighs pressed together as she revved the engine.

"Minx," he said with an unhappy tone, letting her know he knew what she was doing. She laughed and threw her head back, the little jewel on her nose sparkling.

Soon, they reached the restaurant. Gentleman that he was, he opened the door for himself and then helped her out. Tucking her hand into his arm, they walked into the restaurant. The maître d' took his name and led them to their table.

"Do you eat a lot of French food in Lykos?" Kate asked as she perused the menu.

"We eat different kinds of food," he said. "The island itself is like a self-contained city. Similar to Blackstone in some ways. We have our own restaurants, shops, services, even a fire department and a hospital, of course."

"Wow," she said. "Sounds like an interesting place."

"Perhaps someday we could go back." But not for a long while. There was nothing much left for him there after all.

"I'd like that. I've never left the U.S. We mostly went camping for family vacations, and I only went to school over at Colorado U."

The waiter came back and took their orders, then promised to come back with the wine they requested.

"I must admit, Blackstone is turning out to be much more than I expected," he said. "I don't think I've ever lived in or even know of a place where different shifters live together in harmony. There are a few other types of shifters in Lykos, but they are there mostly to work."

"Well, it's not some Utopia here," she said, taking a sip of her water. "But yeah, it's unique. Lucas Lennox, the founder of the town and Sybil's great-great-great-great-grandfather, wanted Blackstone to be a sanctuary of sorts for all shifters.

He declared any shifter who came here to contribute to the community would be under the protection the Blackstone dragons as well as their children and children's children." Her eyes lowered. "You know, my parents weren't from here. I was the only one in my family born in Blackstone."

"I did not know that." Intrigued, he leaned forward. "Tell me more."

"Ma and Pop came from Texas. They were living a quiet, peaceful life in a small town, but someone outed them as wolf shifters," she explained. "And well, a mob came in the middle of the night and drove them off. They took what they could, put Nathan in their truck, and drove out here because they heard Blackstone would welcome wolf shifters like them."

"They were right," Petros said.

"Yeah. And extremely lucky," she added. "They were on their way here and saw Aunt Riva—that's Sybil's mom—stuck on the side of the road after she'd been in an accident. They helped her get back to the castle and well, the rest is history."

"I had no idea," he said. It seemed odd that their family histories were almost similar. His own biological parents were trying to find a better life for him when they escaped the mainland. But perhaps, this was fate working again.

The waiter came with their wine and poured them each a glass after Petros had nodded in approval. They chatted amiably, mostly talking about her work and clients, in only the most Kate way possible. He enjoyed hearing her talk openly. He did not find her cursing crass at all but rather refreshing in a world where most people pretended to be something they were not. No, his Kate was the real thing.

When the evening was winding down, they left, with Kate driving him back to Lennox Corp. so he could take his truck back to his hotel. She pulled up right next to his vehicle.

"So," Kate began as they exited the Mustang. "Are you sure I can't convince you to come back to my place for a nightcap?"

Oh, she was a temptress, but Petros reigned in his desires. "I would like nothing more, but as I said, I shall court you properly."

Kate walked over to his side, her hips swaying gently. "Do I get a good night kiss at least?"

He chuckled. "Of course." He leaned forward, trapping her against the door of his truck. Her arms snaked around his neck and pulled him down, and she pressed her lips to his. She tasted sweet as always, but what she was doing with her body was decidedly not so. Her breasts pressed up against his chest, and she squirmed her hips up at him, brushing against his crotch. His cock instantly reacted, though if he were honest with himself, he'd been half hard throughout their entire date.

She purred with pleasure against his mouth and ground against him. Petros allowed himself to enjoy the sensation of her body against his for a few more seconds before pulling away.

"Kate," he said in a warning tone.

"Oh, you spoilsport," she said with a pout. "So, buddy, before we go any further, I think we need to negotiate the terms."

"Terms?"

"Yes. About when you're gonna put out." She planted her hands on her hips. "I can't make all the time and effort into looking like this knowing it's not working."

"Oh, it's working," he said, as his eyes wandered up and down her delicious body. "But, like I said, I want you to be sure."

"So ... three dates?" she asked.

"At least."

Kate muttered something about "pigs" and "sausages" under her breath that he didn't catch. "Fine. But I'm keeping track." She wagged her finger at him.

He laughed. "Of course. Now," he kissed the wrinkle between her brows, "should I drive back with you and make sure you get home safe?"

"What? Nah, get some rest," she said. "I'm a big girl; I'll be fine."

His wolf told him no, to make sure their mate was safe in her den before going home, but he wanted to respect her wishes. "All right, but send me a message when you're home safe."

"I will," she said. She turned to her car, opened the door, and got inside, then rolled down the windows. "I'll see you tomorrow night? I'll be at The Agency offices in the morning, but I have to go check the systems at the mines in the afternoon."

He was not comfortable with her being surrounded with so many males in one place, but she'd been doing it for years so he had to trust her. "Should I pick you up at your home?"

"Around seven?"

He nodded.

"See you then." She waved at him as she pulled out of her spot and drove out.

He watched the car until it exited the lot and disappeared down the road. Tonight was a success, and he felt confident that Kate would soon be his bonded mate. He had no doubt now.

As Petros walked over to the driver's side, he stopped in his tracks. His wolf's hackles raised, and he heard alarm bells in his head. His instincts had been finely honed over the years, and he knew when he was being watched.

He whipped around. A movement from behind the line of trees caught his attention. Might have been a stray animal. He tried to tune his ears for any sound but didn't hear anything else. Unfortunately, that wasn't a good sign. If it was an animal, it would have made some sound. No, someone had been there. Watching him. No, watching *them*. A shifter most likely, but who? Blackstone was full of shifters; it could have been anyone. Perhaps it was just some resident, out for a moonlit shift to let his or her animal out.

Petros' gaze went back toward the road. Kate was long gone by now. Even a shifter on foot wouldn't have been able to catch up to her, especially the way she drove. But just to be sure, he waited in the parking lot, phone in hand.

Fifteen minutes passed by, and he received a text message.

I'm home.

Good, he replied. He climbed into his truck, but the sound of another message coming in made him pause. When he checked it, he let out an audible groan. It was a selfie of Kate lying in bed wearing only a silky black nightie with a caption underneath: *Change your mind yet? ;)*

Petros grinned to himself and sent a message. *Three dates.*

Spoilsport. Goodnight :)

Sweet dreams, he replied and put the phone away. The little minx could try all she wanted, but he had the patience and discipline of a monk.

Especially when it came to getting what he wanted.

Perhaps he underestimated his mate too much. Kate certainly

would test the patience of a monk. No wait; she would test the patience of a saint.

It seemed innocent enough when she came in the day after their first date, flashing him a naughty smile as she walked by his office on her way to her cubicle. A few minutes later, he received a text message from her saying there was a problem in the server room that needed his attention.

As soon as he walked in, she pinned him against the wall. They had a quick make-out session, and while he wanted to continue, he had to stop before he broke his promise. She seemed disappointed, but the twinkle in her eye said she was not going to give up.

And she didn't, not even when he had to cancel their second date, or attempted to, anyway. He had to work overtime since Luke and Georgina's wedding was only two days away, and they were still making preparations as details came in.

"Oh no way, mister," she had said over the phone as she drove back from the mines later that day. "I'm coming back, and we're going to have date number two."

So, over Chinese takeout in his office, they had their second date. He was checking the positions of the guard teams around the castle, and she planted herself on the desk, eating from the takeout boxes but not before making sure he had eaten as well. She would pick up pieces of sweet and sour pork or broccoli beef and offer it to him as he worked.

"Gotta keep your strength up," she said with a cheeky smile.

They ended the date much in the same way as their first since their original plans of him picking her up fell through. Because of all the attention the security at the wedding demanded of his time, Petros had nearly forgotten about the incident in the parking lot. This time, as he watched Kate drive away, he didn't feel anyone watching him. The incident faded away in his mind.

Besides, he had other things to worry about. First, the wedding was tomorrow, and there weren't nearly enough people to secure it. Holding it on the castle grounds made it simpler, and Ari Stavros would be coming with more people, which would help. But the staff was spread so thin that even he was going to have his own quadrant of the grounds to patrol.

Second, of course, was that tonight would be his and Kate's third date. He wanted her badly. Despite his stipulations, he would have gladly taken her to bed that very first date or even before then, when she marched into Argo's. He still could not believe she had come after him like that. Her actions had hurt him deeply, but the fact that she was willing to swallow her pride and apologize told him Kate was a good person. And he was more than sure she was the only woman for him, but did she feel the same way about him or would it only be sex for her? That's why he had to be sure, because once he made love to her, he knew he would never want another woman again.

"Petros?"

He looked up from his desk. Kate stood by the doorway. "Are you done for the day?"

"Yes, I am," he said as he stood up. "Shall we take your car or mine?"

"I had Sybil drop me off this morning," she said, her smile oddly shy. "I figured it might be easier to just take one car tonight than have to go back and forth."

"Good." He saw her pupils dilate and the flush on her cheeks. They both knew it was inevitable, but the anticipation was thrilling. How long could they draw this out before their desire for one another took over? "Where would you like to go for dinner? I thought it should be ladies' choice tonight."

"How about something familiar? Rosie's if they're not too crowded?"

"Whatever you wish," he said.

They left the office and he drove them down to Main Street. Despite it being the dinner rush, Rosie's wasn't as busy as it had been the last couple of days. They only had to wait five minutes before they were seated in a corner booth. Much to his surprise, Kate slid into the seat beside him.

"Much cozier, right?" she said.

"Much," he replied.

The waitress took their order and left them alone.

"How are the preps for tomorrow's event?" she asked. "Think there's going to be any trouble?"

"Our intelligence says The Organization is in chaos at the moment, and any strike back is unlikely," he began. "But Christina and Jason do not want to take any chances."

She nodded in agreement. "Good."

There was something else weighing on his mind. It was like an itch that began as a small irritation but somehow buried itself in his brain. The feeling that he was being watched was back. Right now, he swore he could feel eyes on him. He glanced around, but nothing seemed out of the ordinary.

"What's wrong?" she asked, frowning at him.

"What? Oh, nothing." He was being paranoid. That incident in the parking lot was nothing. Just a coincidence. He glanced at Kate, her gorgeous face looking up at him and her sweet scent teasing him, he knew there were more important things to think about.

"Petros," she said, her lashes lowering and her voice growing hoarse. "Tonight—"

"We will have plenty of time for tonight later," he said. "But," he nodded to the waitress approaching them with a tray, "for now, let's eat."

The waitress put their food down and wished them a good meal before she left. Kate dug in heartily to her meal—again, another trait he found endearing. He knew many women who wouldn't eat in front of their dates for fear of looking unladylike, but Kate ate her chicken pot pie with gusto.

"How about dessert?" the waitress asked as she came back to clear their meals.

"I already have dessert waiting for me," Kate said with a saucy grin and a wink at Petros.

The waitress laughed. "I'll get your check."

When the young woman walked away, Petros slipped his arm around Kate's waist and pulled her against his side. "Are you sure, Kate?" he whispered in her ear. "You remember what I said about no going back?"

She looked up at him with those beautiful emerald green eyes. "Very sure."

His wolf howled in delight, and he could feel Kate's wolf join in a duet that stirred something deep inside him. He could not wait a single second more. Slapping a large bill on the table, he ushered Kate out of the booth and practically dragged her out of the cafe.

"My hotel is closer," he said as they walked to his truck.

"Let's go there, then."

With all the businesses opening, they had to park farther out, two blocks from Main Street. Not all the lights were functioning on this side of the street, but it didn't matter because his shifter vision would adjust.

"Petros," she began. "I—"

He had been so wrapped up in Kate that he didn't hear the sound of paws thundering toward them until it was too late. He howled in pain as he felt the claws dig deep down his back, but he managed to push Kate away.

"Run!" he urged his mate as he turned around. A large, furry beast pounced on him, knocking him to the ground.

"Petros!" Kate cried. "Mother—"

The wolf growled in his ear, and Petros's own animal was rearing to get out. He called on his wolf to defend him and his mate, and the animal broke free of his skin. He swatted the other wolf away easily and rolled upright.

The other wolf yelped in surprise but managed to stay on its feet. As his vision began to adjust and focus on his attacker, a sickening feeling began to grip him. Petros finally saw the wolf clearly. Familiar, but there was something different about it. He was frozen in shock when he recognized the wolf.

No.

It couldn't be.

But he was—

The wolf leapt at him, claws reaching out toward him, and there was no time to evade. But the attack he was bracing himself for never came as another blur from his right appeared from nowhere and knocked the other wolf down.

No! Petros shouted from inside his wolf. *Kate!*

He had to save Kate. The two wolves rolled around, vying for dominance. The other wolf was much larger, but Kate had the element of surprise. Her wolf opened its mouth and latched onto a leg, biting down so hard the other wolf yowled in pain. Kate used the chance to twist away though she did not run. Her wolf let out a growl and approached the other wolf who was now getting to its feet.

Petros pushed his body and leapt at the wolf before Kate could do anything. As their bodies tangled, he breathed in the other wolf's scent, confirming his worst fears. *No*, he told his wolf, *don't kill him!* He could sense Kate behind them, rearing and ready to go. But he couldn't let her, not when her wolf's thirst for blood was evident.

It seemed like a miracle, but Petros managed to end up on top. "Stop!" he managed to growl out through his wolf's mouth. It seemed like it only angered the other wolf. *Please*, he thought, *don't make me do this.*

The other wolf was in a frenzy, snapping its teeth as him even as it was obviously defeated. In his attempt to not hurt it, the other wolf managed to swipe his claws at his front. Pain bloomed in his chest, and he could feel the sticky sensation of blood on his fur. The wolf pushed him away and as Petros rolled to his side, he watched helplessly as it ran away, disappearing into the tree line. It can't ... but it was *him*. He knew that scent anywhere. But how?

"Petros!" Kate's human voice startled him out of his thoughts. As she knelt beside him, he pushed his wolf inside, reclaiming his body as his own dark fur receded into his skin and his wolf limbs turned back to human ones. "Petros," she said in a broken voice.

"I ... I am fine," he managed to choke out. "My wounds are already healing." He could feel the skin on his back and chest knitting together.

Kate helped him to his feet. "I know, but for a second I thought ...."

He pulled her against him and held her close. Being with his mate relaxed him and calmed his wolf. "Are you hurt?"

"No, not a scratch," she said, sniffing against this chest.

"What the hell happened? Was it a stray wolf? A shifter gone feral?"

Petros wished it was some stray. But he knew who it was. He didn't know how it was possible, but he was one hundred percent sure. "It wasn't."

"Then what was it?"

A pit began to form in his stomach, and the pounding in his ears wouldn't stop. "It was Milos."

Kate stiffened in his arms. "Milos—wait. Your friend? But you said he was dead!"

"That's what we thought." Obviously, they were wrong.

"Are you sure?"

"I'm positive." He had known Milos since they were seven years old. That scent was so distinct, so buried in his mind, that he would never forget it. "He must have survived somehow."

"But why did he attack you if you're his friend?"

Petros shrugged. "Perhaps he's gone feral." That had to be it. Milos had lost his mind and his wolf. They said feral shifters didn't know their own mind and would attack anyone, even friends and loved ones. "We must go to Christina and Jason and tell them."

Kate nodded. "Give me your keys." She held up her hand when he tried to protest. "No! It will give you time to heal. I swear to God, you say anything and I'll drag you to the hospital right now!"

He gave her a weak smile. "I wouldn't expect any less." His mate was fierce, as he'd known all along, and he knew it was no use arguing with her.

They walked over to his truck, and he took the spare set of clothes from the back as Kate slipped her dress back on. The wounds were already closed, but he felt exhausted both physically and mentally, and was glad he didn't have to drive on top of that. As they made their way to Jason and Christina's loft in South Blackstone, it gave him time to close his eyes and think about what just happened.

Milos was alive. The best friend he thought was dead was still living. But what happened to him? Where had he been all this time? Why did he not try to go back to Lykos? And how did he get to Blackstone? He already had a suspicion. As he ran through all the possible scenarios, they all led back to one thing: The Organization. He knew they were all connected, and when he found out who was responsible for all this, he was going to tear them apart with his bare hands.

"We're here," Kate announced as she cut the engine. "I've already sent a message to Jason. They know we're coming."

He followed Kate to the first building on the right and into the elevator. When they reached the top floor, the lone door in the hallway swung open.

"Come in," Jason said, his face serious. He let them inside their spacious loft. They walked inside, and Christina was already seated on the couch.

"Are you all right?" Christina's face was drawn into a look of concern.

Kate sank down on the couch, but Petros remained standing. "We were attacked."

"By who?" Jason asked, his fists clenching at his sides.

"It was Milos."

"Milos? Vasilakis?" Christina's brows knitted together. "But he's dead."

"Apparently not." Petros relayed the story of the attack to them. "… And then he ran away."

"You're sure?" Christina got to her feet. "You didn't see him in human form, though?"

"I didn't need to," Petros said. "I could scent him. It was him, Christina. I know it."

"But how—"

"How else?" he said, cutting her off.

Christina's face turned grim. "You think The Organization got to him?"

"Who knows what they've accomplished with all their experiments?" Petros said.

Jason nodded in agreement. "It's highly possible. Just think about what we've discovered so far."

"This is distressing." Christina tapped a finger on her chin. "I'm going to call HQ in Lykos. I think my father and Kostas are already on the way here for the wedding, but Nikos or Xander should be on-call."

"We should get to work on finding out who did this," Petros said. "And if Milos is out there—"

"I'll inform P.D. and the Rangers," Jason said.

"And I shall call our office and—"

"The only thing you have to do is go home and get rest," Christina said in a firm voice. "No buts, that's an order. I can handle contacting our guys. We still have the wedding tomorrow."

Ah yes, he almost forgot. With these new developments, it could mean the wedding would not be as secure as they thought. "Of course."

"Go and let us handle things," Jason said. "Get your head on straight."

Kate stood up, walked to him, and slipped her hand into his, threading their fingers together. The move was oddly soothing. "I'll get him home," she said.

"You take care. Call us for anything."

"Will do," she said, tugging him toward the exit.

Neither said a word as they left the loft. Petros' mind was racing with all the possibilities. But most of all, he thought of his friend. What could have happened to him to make him turn feral? Was there a possibility of him turning back? Because there was only one way to deal with shifters whose animal sides have taken over, and he did not want to lose his friend for a second time.

Was Milos truly lost?

He glanced down at his and Kate's linked hands. Milos tried to hurt his mate. If he tried to do it again, it would be unforgivable. She was his world now, his number one priority. He would do whatever it took to protect her, no matter what it cost him.

CHAPTER TEN

KATE TOOK a sidelong glance at Petros as they stood inside the elevator that was bringing them down to the lobby. Her heart hurt so much for him, and she could feel how confused and distressed he was. Her wolf was urging her to take action, but she already knew she had to do something about it. As she curled her fingers around his, she gave him a reassuring squeeze.

The elevator chime dinged softly, announcing their arrival. He led them out, still hand in hand, then walked toward his parked truck. When she stopped in her tracks, he gave her a puzzled look.

"Wait," she said.

"What is it?" he asked.

"Don't leave."

He frowned. "I'm not leaving Blackstone."

"No, I mean," she nodded to the identical building beside Jason's, "I live there. At Nathan and Violet's place. Stay with me tonight."

His expression was that of confusion. "Kate, I don't think—"

She gave a little chuckle. "Aww, are you afraid I'm going to jump you?" she asked, trying to inject some humor into the situation. "It's just more practical, okay? We're already here. You don't have to drive back to your hotel and then back to HQ and then the castle tomorrow. You can get a full night's sleep and be ready. Nathan has tons of clothes; I'm sure he won't mind if you borrowed some." She paused. "If you like, we can go back upstairs. Jason can let you crash on their couch—"

"No," he said with a nod. "You're right."

Kate led him to the building, and they took the elevator to the top floor. Nathan's loft was exactly identical to Jason's except for the decor and furnishings. She opened the door and let him inside.

"The bedroom upstairs is Nathan and Violet's. Mine," she pointed to the hallway, "is the one at the end, but there are two other rooms you can choose from. I'll get you some clothes."

Petros gave her a grateful nod and headed toward the bedrooms. She went up to the loft and grabbed a couple of sleep shirts as well as clothes for tomorrow for Petros from Nathan's closet.

As she walked back to the guest rooms, she saw the door to the left one open and went inside. Petros was standing in the middle of the room, unmoving. His shoulders sagged, and his head hung low.

Kate yearned to soothe him as his pain seemed to radiate toward her. Placing the clothes on the dresser, she walked up to him and wrapped her arms around his waist from behind.

As she pressed her cheek to his back to inhale his scent, his body relaxed.

"Do you want to talk?" she murmured.

"No." He gently pried her hands away and turned to face her. "I don't need to talk about anything."

Kate could feel him withdrawing from her. She couldn't let that happen, not when he was obviously in anguish. "Petros." When he tried to move away from her, she held onto his wrists. "No. Don't pull away from me."

"It's not—"

"No!" she said in a firm voice. With a soft sigh, she moved a hand up his chest, to his neck, and cupped his jaw. "Don't." Snaking her hand to the back of his head, she pulled him down for a kiss.

He seemed frozen for a moment, but with her coaxing he began to respond. Tentative at first, but his hesitation seemed to disappear. His kisses became urgent, his thrusting tongue forcing her lips open. It sent her senses reeling, and heat spread through her. She began to nudge him back toward the bed.

"Kate, you don't have to do this." His voice was rough with need. "Not for me."

"I'm not. I mean, yes I'm doing it for you, but also for me." She pushed him down on the bed and stepped back. Slowly, she shrugged off her leather jacket and let it drop to the floor, then slipped her shirt over her head. Petros' blue-green eyes grew dark with desire, his stare never leaving hers. When she was fully bare in front of him, he reached out to her.

His palm was rough and sent electricity across her skin as he snaked it around her waist. With a quick jerk, he pulled her to bed, and she somehow found herself underneath his warm body, pressed up against the hard planes of skin and muscle.

She sighed before his lips claimed hers. His kisses were rough and urgent, and she succumbed to him, letting him do what he wanted. Pushing his tongue inside her, tasting her. Owning her.

She whimpered when his mouth left hers, but then gasped as he bent down to her bare breasts. The shock of his warm and wet tongue on her nipples shot straight to her core, and wetness flooded between her legs. He must have smelled her arousal because he drew the nipple inside deeper, eliciting a sharp cry from her mouth.

He pulled away, his head moving down, lips running over her belly, and lower ...

"Petros!" She bucked her hips up to meet his tongue as it thrust inside her. There was no reason to wait or tease her; she was already dripping wet, and she wanted this badly.

She squirmed and moved her hips up. When he replaced his tongue with his fingers and his mouth found her clit, she cried out and shoved her fingers into his scalp. He stroked her nub with his tongue, sending her body quivering as pleasure crashed through her.

She didn't even have time to catch her breath as he did it again, lashing his tongue against her clit until she was shuddering with a second stronger orgasm.

Her body was still trembling as he moved over her. Gathering what she could from her scrambled brain, she hooked a leg around his and leveraged his weight so she wound up on top of him.

His cock was already hard through his pants, pressing up against her. She flashed him a wicked smile and licked her lips. Desire clouded his eyes and he remained still, waiting for her to make her move.

"Off," she ordered, pulling his shirt from his pants. He

made quick work of the buttons and shrugged off the offending garment. Meanwhile, she worked on unzipping his pants and pulling them down to his thighs along with his underwear.

Kate sucked in a breath as his stiff cock bobbed in front of her, and she bit her tongue as she looked at the monumental task at hand. She'd seen him naked earlier when he shifted back, but not like this. She wrapped a hand around it, gently squeezing and enjoying the feel of velvet over steel.

He let out a soft curse when she moved her head down to take the tip in her mouth. She closed her eyes, breathing in his musky scent mixed with desire, the blood roaring in her ears reminding her of the ocean where he had come from. It was heady, and her desire seemed to increase as she gave him pleasure with her tongue, something she'd never felt before. Pushing her head down, she took as much of him as she could and sucked back, teasing him with her tongue.

"Kate-mine," he rasped. "I cannot—"

She nodded and popped him out of her mouth, then crawled over him. Placing her knees on either side of his hips, she lowered herself onto his cock. Slowly, leisurely, she sank down on him, allowing herself to adjust to his girth and size. When he bottomed out, she relaxed her body, though she still felt incredibly full.

"You are exquisite," he said, looking up at her. "Kate-mine. My mate."

Kate laid her hands on his chest, tracing up and down his magnificent body, feeling his rock hard abs underneath her fingers. It was hard to believe this man was all hers.

"Kate, please," he said.

She began to move her hips back and forth experimentally to test how he felt inside her. There was no way to describe the way it felt. She leaned back, got on her knees, and began to ride him in earnest. Slow at first, but the sensations inside her were too much, and she rocked her hips faster and faster, feeling that tightness building in her core.

Large hands reached up toward her, cupping her breasts. As Petros rolled her nipples between his fingers, she moved faster as pleasure began to ripple through her body.

"Fuck!" she moaned when he sat up and pulled her to him, taking a nipple into his mouth. She shuddered, her orgasm starting to build in waves. Petros bit her nipple, and *motherfucking hell*, that was enough to push her over the edge. She wept when the pleasure washed over her.

He rolled her over without breaking contact and began to thrust hard into her. She arched up into him as he buried himself in her, over and over again. Desperation set in, despite her earlier orgasms, wanting him deep inside her.

"More," she whispered. "Harder."

He obliged, reaching up to the headboard behind and—fucking hell—changing the angle of his hips just right to hit her clit over and over again. She screamed his name as her strongest orgasm hit her, and she clenched around him as he furiously continued to fuck into her.

He roared his orgasm, his body shaking hard. She felt his cock pulse and empty into her. God, she had never felt so filled and satisfied as when he came. He didn't stop, thrusting and grunting until he was fully spent, finally collapsing on top of her.

She held her breath as he pulled out of her, her body protesting at the loss. He rolled away, and she curled up to her side. The mattress lightened as he got up but dipped again with his weight as he moved up behind her.

Arms pulled her close to a hard chest. "Sleep," he whispered in her ear.

Feeling content and satisfied, she closed her eyes and allowed sleep to take over.

Kate's eyes fluttered open, the light hitting her eyelids slowly waking up her confused brain. For a second, she thought last night was a dream, but the delicious soreness between her legs told her it wasn't.

"Petros, I—" She stopped when she rolled over, her hands seeking out his body. But all she got were cool sheets and the trace scent of ocean and earth.

She breathed in deep. Sex with Petros was earth-shattering, to say the least. Why had she resisted all this time? She had never felt like this, never felt so right so deep in her bones.

But where was he?

A ringing sound made her jolt up in bed. The sound was faint, and she couldn't find her phone.

"Oh!" She lunged toward the floor where she had discarded her jacket. Fishing her phone from the front pocket, she answered it. "Hello."

"Kate, where the heck are you?" Sybil's voice burst through the speakers.

"Uh, at home?"

"Do you have any idea what time it is? Aunt Laura's been waiting since seven a.m."

She looked around and saw the number on the bedside clock. *Yikes.* It was nearly noon, and Luke and Georgina's wedding was in four hours. She was supposed to help Aunt

Laura, Amelia, and Sybil with the set up and decor, since the couple didn't want to hire any outside vendors for fear of having another security breach. "Sorry! I slept in."

Sybil snorted. "I'm sure there was a lot of sleeping happening."

Kate walked over to the bathroom and yanked the shower door open. "What? Who told you?"

"You did," she said. "Remember, you were texting me the whole day about how last night was date number three? And you were finally going to 'get the D'?"

"Oh, yeah."

"Well? How was it? I mean—wait! No dirty details!"

"But those are the best parts," she said as she turned on the tap. "It was … I'll tell you when I get there okay? Give me thirty minutes."

"All right but not a minute longer!"

Kate put the phone down on the counter and stepped into the shower, letting the warm spray soothe her aching muscles. Hmm, it felt amazing, but her mind wandered to where Petros could be. A nagging thought was burrowing in her brain, but she dismissed it. Sure, she was used to sneaking out of some guy's bed or waking up alone, but this was different.

"Ah-ha!" She remembered how tied up Petros had been with the wedding arrangements. He probably had to leave early. Christina would tear him a new one if he was late, plus there was the possibility of The Organization striking back at them. *That was it*, she thought as she squeezed some shampoo into her hair. All doubts left her mind.

She'd see him at the wedding, and maybe when he was off-duty, they could come back here and have some more fun sexy times.

CHAPTER ELEVEN

Petros' eyes scanned the area just behind the back lawn of Blackstone Castle. He was close enough so he could hear the cheer of the guests and the music.

"Ceremony's done," a disembodied voice of an agent coming from the comm piece in his ear said.

"Roger," he replied. "Section A, Quadrant B is secured. Send Markos to sweep this area. I need to report back to Christina."

"Roger that."

Petros took one last glance around him and headed toward the castle. How he managed to function at all this morning, he wasn't sure. Leaving Kate had been difficult, especially watching her sleep as the sun came up. But he had his duty to The Agency. And, his wolf was all fired up, remembering what had transpired the night before. It was screaming at him to protect their mate at all costs.

Even now, the image of Kate and Milos fighting in wolf form was burned into his head. Kate was smart and quick, but in a real fight, no match for Milos. Like Petros, he was trained by the best fighters in Lykos and by the Alpha himself. One wrong move or slip, and Milos's teeth could have sank right into her vulnerable neck.

No! He could not let that happen. Would not let it happen. So, no matter how much the need to stay with her was strong, he knew he had to go. For her sake.

And he knew, if something happened, it would be his fault. Maybe Kate was right; they should have resisted the mating bond. Being with him only put her in danger now. The emotions inside him were brewing to the point of danger. And, like a coward, he slunk away without waking her.

The longer he stayed away from her, the more he realized that was a mistake. By the end of the day, he would seek her out and apologize for leaving her bed.

Petros entered the castle through the side doors that led to the kitchens, then walked toward the ballroom where he knew the cocktails were being served while the staff set up tables and food outside. Christina, who was standing by the bar with Jason, Catherine, and Matthew, waved him over as soon as he entered.

"Everything all right?" Christina asked.

"No incidents or anything to report," he replied.

"Good," Matthew said. "Want a drink, man?"

"No, thank you," he said. "I'm still on duty."

"At least someone is taking their work seriously," Catherine said, nodding toward the middle of the ballroom.

Petros followed her gaze, then frowned with disapproval as he saw who she was referring to. Agatha was standing among a small group, laughing and chatting as she held a drink in her hand. Christina had assigned some of them to mingle amongst the guests, but this was not exactly what she had in mind.

Christina placed her glass of wine on top of the bar. "I'll go and relieve her of her duty."

"No," he said, raising a hand. "Apologies; this is my responsibility." If he hadn't been so distracted the entire week, he would have realized this was the worst place for the young agent. She was becoming entirely way too comfortable in Blackstone. "I'll take care of this. Please, enjoy the celebration."

With a final nod to the foursome, he turned on his heel and strode toward Agatha. He clenched his jaw, trying to tamp down the anger building inside him. There was a real threat out there, and here she was risking their lives so she could socialize with Blackstone's elite.

"Explain yourself," Petros said as he came up behind Agatha. Discretely, he took her elbow and tugged her away from the circle of people. He dragged her to the nearest empty alcove.

"What the f—oh!" Her face went as red as the scandalously low cut dress she was wearing. "Petros! I was only doing my duty."

"Your duty is to protect the people here, not to act like some society heiress," he ground out.

Agatha pouted. "You said we had to blend in," she purred, rubbing a hand down his chest. "And so I followed your orders." Something in her expression changed, and, looking back, he should have known better. "Oh Petros," she said, her voice pitching higher. "Yes, please!" She threw herself at him so fast, he didn't have time to evade her. "Now that you're done with her, we can finally be together."

What the hell? Petros tried to pry Agatha's limbs off him, but she was using her shifter strength to hold on to him.

"You. Asshole."

Kate's voice cut right into him, and he knew there was going to be trouble. He used all his might to remove Agatha's arms from him and pushed her away. He prayed it wasn't too late and turned to face his mate.

Kate's face was scarlet, all the way to the tips of her ears. She stood there, chest heaving as she turned her hate-filled gaze from Agatha to him.

"Kate-mine—"

"Shut up!" She held up a hand. "So, that's it, huh? That's why you left this morning after screwing me last night?"

"What?" Shock and anger coursed through his system.

"Petros," Agatha purred. "Tell her the truth. That you've been toying with her as a joke—"

"She is my mate!" he growled. His wolf was furious at the other woman. It didn't care that Agatha was female; it wanted blood for the insult.

"I am not his mate," Kate said. "You want him? You can have him!"

"Kate!" He tried to grab her, but she evaded him easily and ran across the room. He wanted to go after her and knock some sense into her, but the people in the room were already beginning to stop and stare at them. Christina was going to be livid if he ruined her brother-in-law's wedding.

"Agatha Agrippina," he said, turning to her. "You are relieved of your duty. Pack your things and take the first flight back to Lykos."

"What!" she screeched. "You can't do that! I'm going to complain—"

"To whom?" he asked. "To the Alpha? He's right over there. Go ahead."

Ari Stavros was standing in the far corner with Hank and

Riva Lennox, his sharp eyes trained at them, a look of disapproval on his face.

Petros nodded to one of the agents and signaled for them to come over. "Escort Miss Agrippina back to her hotel room and assist her in packing her things."

He didn't bother staying. There may be some fallout, but he could deal with that later. Right now, he had to find his mate.

He walked in the direction she had stormed off to and saw a flash of pink hair by the door and turn a corner.

"Kate!" he called as he saw her running down the corridor. That only seemed to fuel her, and she ran faster. Gritting his teeth, he chased after her, nearly bumping into a petite figure wearing white. It was a good thing Luke Lennox had fast reflexes and was able to pull his bride away.

Kate stopped and then shrieked. "I said stay away from me!"

"How could you say those words to me?" he said. "After last night? You could think I would even *look* at another woman?"

"I don't care what you do! Just leave me alone from now on."

"You can't mean that, Kate-mine," he said, stalking toward her slowly. He was scared she would run again.

"And what are you going to do about it?" she challenged, even as he backed her against the wall. "I—EEEKK!"

The damn woman wouldn't listen again, so he did what he had to do—pick her up and take her away from here.

"You, you—*troglodyte*! Put me down this instant!" She kicked her legs violently.

Petros turned to look back at Luke and Georgina, who was standing there, stunned. "Congratulations," he said. "And apologies. We'll be leaving now so as not to cause any more disruptions to your wedding."

"Uh, thanks?" Georgina said.

Petros ignored Kate's protests and instead hurried his pace as he spotted the door at the end of the hallway. He set Kate down and locked the door behind him.

"How dare you?" she said, running to the other end of the small room and pressing herself against the dresser propped up against the wall. "I can't believe you did that again!"

"It's because you won't listen, you infuriating woman!" After all this, surely his anger was justified. "I would have thought last night meant something to you."

"Of course it did!" she said. "But you left this morning! Without saying goodbye."

He knew that had been a mistake. But how to tell her? "Kate-mine." He approached her carefully. "Remember what I said? Once we make love, there would be no going back." There was a tightness in his chest, and he feared he would burst from all the emotions he was feeling. "After last night, I couldn't … I had to protect you. And my first instinct was to run. To ensure that Milos would never be near you again."

"Petros …."

He had failed her. He knew this. "When I saw you with Milos, it tore me up inside. I should be the one protecting you. Fighting for you."

"That's bullshit," she said. "Mates protect each other."

He gave her a weak smile. "It was my mistake thinking leaving you was for your own good. I also realized, well, all this time I'd been single-minded in my pursuit of you. I thought it was fate that led me here and to you, and things would just fall into place. But that was selfish of me. After all, what place did I have in your life? I have nothing to offer you, nor am I worthy of you—"

"Stop! You stupid man!" She lunged at him, pressing her lips to his. "Please stop talking like that."

"What would you have me say then, Kate-mine?" He was already lifting her up and placing her on top of the dresser.

"I—Oh God! Please!" His fingers were already between her thighs, pressing up against her heat. The front of her panties dampened instantly with her desire, and her sweet scent wrapped around him. "More."

He slipped a hand under her panties, thrusting his fingers inside her. "I can't wait," he said, using his other hand to unbuckle his belt.

"Then don't," she replied as her hand grabbed the back of his head and pulled him down for a kiss.

He groaned against her lips and then yanked her panties aside and thrust his already engorged cock into her in one move. She threw her head back and yelped as her pussy clasped around him, sheathing him in her tight, wet warmth. Her arms wound around him, and she pressed her face against his neck, whimpering from pleasure as he moved inside her.

"Kate … Kate …." He said her name over and over again, in rhythm with his thrusting. His mind was filled with just her. Nothing else mattered in this moment, only his mate. He bit his lip as he felt her body tense and clamp around him even harder. He held on as long as he could, waiting for her orgasm to course through her. As she was shuddering, he let go, crying her name out one last time as he spurted his seed into her. Her legs tightened around him, pushing him deeper inside her.

His heartbeat slowed down somewhat, but the blood pumping through his veins was still racing through his body.

Slowly, he backed away and pulled his softening cock out of her. Seeing her like this, her dress hiked to her waist, his cum on her thighs, and a look of pure satisfaction plastered on her face was enough to make his heart pound again.

"Wow," she said. "I think make-up sex is the best."

"Don't think we will be fighting all the time," he warned her.

Kate pulled her dress down and hopped off the dresser. "I told you I'm not some meek mouse who's going to agree with you all the time."

"Oh no." He pulled her to him, inhaling her scent. "I would never mistake you for meek."

She sank against him. "Can you get out of here? If not now, then before the reception ends?"

"I think that can be arranged."

CHAPTER TWELVE

"I ... HOW MUCH ... TIME ...."

"Fifteen minutes," Petros groaned, pressing his forehead to hers.

"Okay, why are you stopping then?" Kate said, giving him a saucy grin.

Petros growled and lifted her up from the table in one swoop.

"Wait, what are you ... oh! Fuck!" Petros pushed her up against the wall. The *fucking* glass wall of his cold-ass office, which meant *her* ass was squished up against the cold window facing the main room. It was a good thing the staff was on their dinner break, but Kate supposed it was entirely her teasing Petros by flashing him her new black lace underwear.

"Oh!" A particularly hard thrust positioned just the right way made her shiver uncontrollably. He bent his head, popped her tit out of her bra, and took a nipple into his mouth, giving her a gentle enough bite that sent her spiraling over the edge. She hoped this wall was strong enough to hold them, otherwise, when the rest of the overnight staff came back, they would be in for a very big surprise.

"Fuck!" She clung onto Petros' shoulders as he moved her back to the table. Flipping her over, he positioned her on her knees, then quickly thrust deep inside her from behind.

"Goddamn!" His fingers dug into her scalp, tugging at it with just the right amount of force that had her moaning. He pulled her back up, all the while thrusting into her like a madman. Fuck, her knees were going to regret this in the morning, but it was just too good.

His hold tightened around her. "Just one more, Kate-mine," he said. "Be a good girl and come for me one more time."

Fucking hell. She hoped there was no such thing as death from too much sex because it would be an embarrassing way to go. But, decidedly not the worst.

His teeth sank into her shoulder, a move that sent her howling. He covered her mouth to muffle her screams, and as her body convulsed into one last powerful orgasm, she swore she saw stars. Petros let out a guttural cry as he came, his cock pulsing inside her.

When her vision finally returned, she looked up at the clock behind Petros' desk. "Five minutes to spare," she said as she scrambled off the table. Petros was already zipping up his pants as she pulled her panties up and smoothed her dress down. "Thanks for dinner, babe," she said, kissing him on the cheek.

"We did not even get to eat it," he said, glancing at the brown paper bag on the floor.

"I'm fine," she said. "I'm very ... satisfied."

Petros laughed. "I'm sure you are." He pulled her close to

him. "I wish I did not have to stay. I do not like being away from you."

"Me neither," she said. "But these overnight shifts are part of the job, right?"

He placed his chin on top of her head. "I'm afraid so."

"Bummer." She sighed. "Well, I guess I'll head home then."

"I'll bring you some breakfast," he promised, kissing her forehead.

"You better," Kate retorted. "And then some morning sex?"

"You're insatiable," he chuckled.

"*Excuse* me," she said. "But I still have rug burns *on top* of my rug burns." Since the wedding, almost every spare second they had were spent wrapped around each other in bed. Or the shower. Or the kitchen. And then there was the janitor's closet yesterday….

"I can't help it," he said in a low, raspy voice. "I just need to be inside you all the time." His fingers slid down to her ass.

"Hmm." It was like his mere touch could send her pussy gushing with wetness. "Petros—"

The sound of the door opening made them jump apart. The staff was back, which meant they had to look professional. Of course everyone already knew they were sleeping together, so it didn't really matter, but Kate knew it was important for Petros to command the respect of his people.

"I really should go. It's been a long day, and I'm interviewing with a new client tomorrow."

"You are?" he asked.

"Yeah. I've been following up for months but looks like they're ready to deal," she said.

His face lit up. "Excellent. I'm happy for you."

"Petros, it's only an initial chat," she said.

"But still, I'm proud of you," he said, smiling at her warmly.

Her heart melted into a puddle. When was the last time a guy told her that or was even interested in her work? Uh, probably … never.

"Thank you." She grabbed her purse and laptop bag from the chair in front of his desk. "I'll see you in the morning."

"I—" He cursed softly when the sound of a call came in from his computer. "That's the Alpha. I forgot we had a video conference scheduled for now. Can you wait for me or should I have Adriano escort you to your car?"

"Don't worry about me," she said. "I'm a big girl." Besides, since the attack on Blackstone, Lennox had secured their headquarters even more.

"But—"

"Go." She nodded to the computer. The ringing had become insistent. "I'll be fine."

He seemed conflicted but nodded and walked over to his chair and put his headphones in. Kate waved goodbye as she left his office.

As soon as she got to her parking spot, Kate got into the Mustang and drove out of the lot, then headed south. Tonight would be the first night since last week that she wouldn't be sleeping next to Petros. It seemed strange, seeing as she'd been sleeping alone most of her life, but she knew the bed would feel cold and empty without him. Still, he'd be bringing her breakfast in the morning, and then they'd have some nookie. Or maybe sex first, depending on her mood. *Sounds like someone's going to have an awesome morning.*

Kate was so distracted she didn't see the figure in the middle of the road until it was too late. It was some kind of animal, at least from what she saw before it went flying, bouncing off the hood of the car and ending up behind her.

She screamed in fright. Slamming down hard on the brakes, she swerved the Mustang to the shoulder. The vehicle jerked to a stop, and she jerked against the seatbelt. Her brain was scrambled in her skull, and it took her a couple of seconds to realize what she had done. What if it was a shifter? She immediately got out of the car.

"Hello?" she called. "Are you okay? Do you need help?"

The sound of a gun cocking and the press of something cold and metal to the back of her head made her freeze.

"Don't move, she-wolf," the voice was rough and the accent heavy, "or I will blow your brains out."

She went still. A direct bullet to the brain was something her enhanced healing could never recover from.

The barrel of the gun moved across the circumference of her head until it landed between her eyes. Kate gasped as her shifter vision adjusted to the darkness, and she saw the man in front of her.

He was tall and well-built, his massive arms like tree trunks. He had dark hair and a scraggly beard. His face could have been called handsome, but he was missing his left eye, which was covered in healed scar tissue. When she drew in a breath, she got a whiff of his scent, and she immediately knew who it was.

"So, you're Petros' bitch."

She gritted her teeth. "You're Milos," she said. "His best friend."

"Was," he said. "I *was* Milos Vasilakis."

"Was?"

"I don't know what I am now," he growled. "But I'm quite certain I'm *not* his friend."

"What do you want?" she asked.

"What do I want?" He pressed the gun harder against her skull. "I want him to suffer! The way I did!"

"Please," she said, her voice trembling. "I can help. We can find you some help."

"Oh, you'll be helping me all right, bitch," he spat. "Helping me get my revenge."

Real fear gripped her entire body. "Revenge? What for? He wasn't the one who hurt you."

"But he was the one who left me behind!" he screamed.

"No! You—"

"No more talking!" He grabbed her arm and dragged her along the shoulder of the road. A few feet away was a rusty old truck. Milos shoved her toward the driver's side. "Get in," he ordered.

With shaky hands, she opened the door and hopped inside. Milos kept his gun trained at her as he crossed over to the passenger side. When he got in, he handed her the keys and pressed the gun to her head. "Drive."

"To where?"

"Just drive, bitch! I'll tell you where to go."

She bit her lip, trying not to cry out in pain as the gun dug deep into her temple. She slipped the key into the ignition. The truck's engine sputtered, then roared to life. Putting the truck in gear, she moved onto the road.

"Milos," she said. "I—"

"Don't call me that!"

"Than what should I call you?"

"They called me Subject 4226," he said in a quiet voice. "But you do not need to call me anything because you will not be around for long."

Oh God. He was insane. Based on what little information she could gather, she guessed The Organization had captured him somehow and conducted experiments on him. No wonder he had gone insane, thinking this was somehow all Petros' fault.

"Take the exit to Highway 79," he ordered, referring to the old road that connected Blackstone and the next town. It was a smart move because 79 was an older highway that was mostly abandoned when the newer freeway system was set up. At this time of night, no one would be driving there.

As they drove down the road, Kate had to find a way to escape, but how? The farther away they got from Blackstone, the lower her chances of getting away from this madman. *Breathe*, she told herself. *You got this*. She had to find a way.

They turned onto 79, and Kate gritted her teeth. Her mind scrambled for a way out of this situation. She was losing hope each second they drove farther away, but then the roar of an engine coming toward them made a lightbulb flash in her brain. *I'm sorry*, she said in a silent prayer.

The single light of the motorcycle coming toward them appeared in the distance. As it drew closer, Kate braced herself and swerved onto the oncoming bike.

"Bitch!" Milos roared, his eyes going wide as the cab filled with light from the oncoming motorcycle. The sound of brakes screeching rang in her ears. Kate brought her elbow up and knocked it against Milos' arm, then slammed on the brakes. She heard the gun hit the windshield, and, knowing this might be her only chance, opened the door and slid out.

She ran, as fast as she could, not caring which direction. The sound of growls and bones popping was right behind her, and she knew the only way she could defend herself was to shift. Her wolf was already rearing to go, but before she could call on it, a large, furry body knocked her down.

"No!" she screamed. She covered her face as the wolf's

razor-sharp teeth snapped at her. Her own wolf was making its appearance, and she could feel her incisors elongating as a growl escaped her throat. But before she could fully transform, she heard a loud guttural growl and then the wolf on top of her was gone.

"What the—"

The wolf was flung ten feet to her right. It whimpered and rolled to its feet, but when it looked at her, its tail suddenly lowered. It turned around and then scampered away.

Kate's heart was still hammering in her chest. What the hell happened? Slowly, she looked up. "Holy shit."

A very large and angry-looking bear was towering over her. No, it wasn't just any bear. It was a polar bear. Nearly twelve feet tall, with massive arms and gigantic paws tipped with black claws. It shook its mammoth head from side to side, let out a snarl, then slowly began to shrink.

Oh no.

Oh hell *no.*

The man standing over her ran his hands down his face and swore. "Hey, are you okay miss—Kate?" Even in the dark, his light blue eyes seemed luminous. "Kate Caldwell?"

Fucking hell.

Of all the fucktards in the world to come rescue her, it *had* to be him. *Mason Fucking Grimes.* Polar bear shifter and all-around supreme jerk.

Kate ignored the hand Mason offered and got to her feet by herself. "What the fuck are you doing here?"

Mason scowled at her. "Saving your life, apparently."

"Yeah, well I was doing fine on my own," she said, wiping her hands down her skirt.

"Didn't seem like it," he said. "You still causing trouble, Caldwell?"

"You still a lying asshole, Grimes?" Kate didn't bother to wait for an answer as she turned her back to him and began to walk away. She didn't have time for this. Milos really was here, and he obviously wanted to get back at Petros for some reason. She had to get back to Blackstone and warn him.

The truck was still on the side of the road. She climbed inside and turned the ignition. Nothing. "Fucking hell." Her purse was back in the Mustang, so she couldn't even call for help.

As she slipped out of the truck, she heard the distinct sound of a Harley coming up behind her. *Shit.*

Mason stopped his hog right beside her. He'd already gotten dressed in his usual getup—knit beanie, white shirt, leather jacket and riding pants. A thick beard covered half his face, and it looked like he needed a trim. "Get on," he ordered, offering her a spare helmet.

"Nuh-uh, no thanks!" She crossed her arms over her chest. "I'd rather walk back to Blackstone."

"Suit yourself," he shrugged. "But that wolf looked really nasty. Wouldn't want to be here when he comes back."

Or what if Milos goes after Petros, a voice said inside her. She had to warn him. "Fuck." She yanked the helmet from him and put it on. "Fine. I just need a ride to Lennox Corp." She went behind him and swung a leg over his ride. "What the hell are you doing back here anyway?"

"Me? I'm moving to Blackstone."

The roar of the Harley muffled the string of curses she hurled at him. He laughed and revved the engine even more as they sped down the highway on their way back to Blackstone.

When they reached Lennox Corp., Mason had barely cut the engine when she hopped off the bike. She had to get to Petros *now*. Who knows what Milos could be planning? She ducked under the barrier gate leading into the building, ignoring the shouts of the guard behind her, and ran straight for the building entrance. As she got closer, relief swept through her as she saw Petros standing out front, speaking to two other agents.

"Petros!" she cried.

He turned toward her, his face changing from serious, to shock, and then relief. "Kate," he rasped when she flung herself in his arms. He immediately pressed his lips to hers in an urgent kiss.

She wanted to melt into him, her body sagging as the adrenaline left her, and she realized how close she had been to dying.

"What happened?" he asked. "You weren't answering your phone and I had someone check on you. We found your car and your purse—"

"It was Milos," she said. "He took me and—"

"Hey, Caldwell!"

Fucker. She disentangled herself from Petros' arms and turned around. "What the fuck are you still doing here?"

Mason strode up to them, his scowl deepening. "You have my helmet."

Kate unbuckled the chin strap and then shoved it at him. "Here you go. Now get the hell away from me."

"You're fucking welcome by the way." He grabbed the helmet. "For, you know, saving your life."

"What is going on?" Petros said, his shoulders squaring. "Kate, who is this man? Did he really save your life?"

Kate answered with a strangled cry that was as close to an affirmative as she could get.

"Mason Grimes," the other man said, offering his hand.

"Petros Thalassa." He took Mason's hand and gripped it tight. "Thank you for saving my mate's life."

"Mate?" Mason's face turned to disbelief, then he let out a laugh. "Seriously?" He looked at Kate and then back at Petros. "Oh man, I don't know if I should say congratulations or sorry."

Kate's clenched her fists. "If you're just going to stand here and insult me, then you should just leave."

Mason raised his hands. "Hey, I just wanted to make sure you were okay. That wolf," he shook his head, "he didn't feel right. He was out for blood. Feral."

Petros tensed up. "I'm very grateful to you, Mr. Grimes—"

"Mason. Just Mason."

Petros nodded. "Mason. I owe you a debt of gratitude."

Mason shrugged. "It's fine. Anyone would have done the same." He glanced at Kate. "Well, almost anyone. I'll see you around then." He pivoted and began to walk away.

"That lying sonofabitch," Kate muttered.

"What's the matter?" Petros asked. "Did he—" He stopped suddenly, his jaw hardening and his mouth setting into a straight line. The silence was deafening between them until he decided to speak. "Kate, is he a former lover?"

"I—what? Oh gross!" The creepy crawlies spread over her arms. "God no!" She gagged. "That *loser* is Amelia's ex!" *Oh God.* "Shit!" If Amelia found out Mason was moving to Blackstone, she might never come home. But if she kept this from Amelia, her friend would never forgive her.

Petros visibly relaxed. "I told you before, the past does not matter to me. However if you—"

She swatted him playfully on the arm. "Green is a good look on you."

He gave her a wry smile, but his expression darkened. "Let's go inside. You need to tell me what happened from the beginning."

CHAPTER THIRTEEN

Now that his mate was here, the maelstrom of emotions inside Petros was finally calming down. His wolf seemed mollified at the sight and smell of her too, and it lay quietly inside him. Still, his wolf was anything but relaxed, and neither was he. No, they would be on alert at all times, at least until they hunted down Milos and put a stop to his madness.

After his video call with the Alpha, Kate had not texted him that she was home. It was strange because she usually had something witty to say or sent him a provocative picture the moment she was in the door. When he called her, Petros tried not to panic when she didn't answer, but his wolf was screaming at him to make sure she was all right. He asked Christina to check if she had come home, and when she said no one answered when she knocked on the door, Petros knew something was wrong.

He sent someone to go to her house, but the agent wasn't even gone five minutes when he got the call. The Mustang was found on the side of the road, the door open, and Kate's things inside. There were no signs of a struggle, but Petros knew Kate would never abandon her brother's car like that. He immediately called Christina, Jason, and all their agents to begin the search.

"Petros, I'm here," she said in a soothing voice. She was planted on his lap as they sat on his chair in his office. His arms were wound around her, unable to let her go.

"I know," he said.

"Then stop growling, yeah?" she said, giving him a weak smile. She placed a hand over his chest and rested her head on his shoulder, which indeed had been rumbling with the unsatisfied growls of his wolf. Her touch soothed his animal, and it quieted down.

"Catch us up with what's happening," Jason said as he and Christina walked into Petros's office.

Kate slipped off his lap but remained at his side, their hands linked. "I was driving home when this animal showed up on the road. I went to check on it and …."

Petros couldn't help the anger building in him as Kate told the story of what happened to her. Hearing for the second time did not tamper his anger; it only fanned the flames. Milos had tried to kill his mate, and he was doing it as revenge. The only way he could describe the torment he was feeling right now was like trying to grasp the blade of a knife. There was no way to make it less painful, no matter which way he positioned his hand. He had to protect his mate from the man who had been like a brother to him growing up, which could mean ending Milos' life. But when the choice came down, he knew which one he would make.

"Wait, how did you overpower him?" Jason asked.

Kate grimaced. "The man on the Harley. Mason Grimes." Her face scrunched into distaste at the name. "Scared Milos off."

"Where have I heard that name ... Tim's nephew?" Jason said, his brows scrunching together. "I remember him. He was here, what, three or four years ago? Stayed the whole summer while he was on leave from the military."

"Don't remind me," Kate said. "Anyway, what are we going to do about Milos?"

"*We* are not going to do anything," Petros said. "*You* will stay out of this. I will handle Milos."

"Just wait a Goddamn minute!" Kate pulled her hand from his and placed it on her hip. "You don't get to tell me what to do! I can help—"

"No!" Petros got to his feet. "I will not have you in harm's way."

"You can't—"

"Stop acting like children, both of you," Christina said. "Calm down. We're dealing with one wolf here. A near-feral wolf, but it's not something The Agency can't handle."

"Christina is right," Jason said. "I'm assuming you want him captured alive and unharmed?"

"If possible." His gut clenched as he looked at Kate and thought of how close he had been to losing her. "But not necessary." If Milos had truly gone feral, then death would be a merciful thing.

"Then we have to try to help him," Christina said in a calm voice. "I'm sure Father would agree. He was one of us, part of our pack, and it is our duty to help him."

Relief swept over Petros. It was one of the rules of the Lykos pack: always care for the sick, the old, and the injured. "We need to draw him out and be ready."

"How do we do that?" Kate asked.

"We give him what he wants," Petros said. "Me."

"No freaking way!" Kate protested. "I'm not letting him get his claws on you!"

"That won't happen," Jason said. "He's on our turf. We can control all the variables."

"Jason is right," Petros said, trying to reassure Kate. "And we need to capture him before he hurts anyone else or himself."

"We need a plan," Jason said.

"It's obvious he's not going to stop until he kills me," Petros said. "But he's also going to start making mistakes."

"He's been observing your movements and striking whenever he sees a vulnerability," Christina said. "First after you guys had dinner at Rosie's and tonight when Kate was alone."

"How can we draw him out then?" Kate asked.

"Milos will strike soon. He knows we're on the lookout for him," Christina said. She tapped her finger on her chin, then her face lit up. "Tomorrow. At the Block Party to celebrate the reopening of Main Street."

"That's tomorrow?" Kate asked, a confused look on her face.

"If you two had come up for some air at some point," Jason said with a knowing smile, "you would have seen all the flyers and signs."

"He won't strike tonight because he knows I'll be on alert," Petros said. "But he will not wait any longer because he knows we'll be closing in on him."

"You should just stay put," Kate said. "Go somewhere secure, and The Agency—"

"Then he will know something is wrong," Petros pointed out. "Milos is much smarter than he seems. He needs to think my guard is down again. We will mingle at the party and look relaxed and carefree."

"But we'll have eyes on him the whole time," Christina said.

"And everyone else?" Jason asked. "What about the people at the party?"

"He won't strike in front of a crowd, especially not a group of shifters, including three dragons," Petros said. "He's crazy but not stupid. I'll leave the party at certain points and attempt to draw him out."

"You mean we'll leave the party." Kate clasped her hand around his. "Together. We can pretend we're going to have a quickie or something."

Petros bit his lip. "All right."

Christina stood up, then clasped her hands together. "All right, inform the team. Let's go to the conference room and work out the details."

Kate nodded at him. "We'll get him, babe. And then you can have your best friend back."

"I know we will." Despite Kate's reassurance, his insides were twisting. While he didn't want to have Milos put down, he was not going to let his mate get hurt again. But if he forbade her from being there, the more she was going to resist. He had to find a way to keep her safe so he could concentrate on catching Milos.

By the time they walked into the conference room, he already had a backup plan forming in his head. He only hoped Kate would forgive him.

CHAPTER FOURTEEN

The Main Street Block Party was in full swing by the time Petros and Kate arrived sometime after dark. Paper lanterns, streamers, balloons, and other festive decor had been set up, and the street and all the businesses had their lights on and doors open to let people inside. Many had also set up booths outside on the sidewalk to sell their goods and refreshments. At the end of the street, there was a stage and a band. It was hard to believe it wasn't too long ago that Hank Lennox stood in his dragon form in the exact same spot and razed the street where The Organization's soldiers and The Chief tried to kill his son, Luke. The entire road had been cleaned and re-paved as if nothing had ever happened.

"Auntie Kate! Auntie Kate!"

A bundle of energy barreled into her legs, nearly knocking Kate over. Little Grayson Mills held his chubby arms up, and she graciously complied. "Hello Grayson! How are you?" She gave him a tight hug and a kiss on the nose, then put him back down on the ground.

"I'm doin' great, Auntie Kate!" he said, looking up at her

with a grin. "I just had some candy apples and cotton candy and corn dogs, then we went to see the clowns …."

As Grayson continued his story, Petros alternated his gaze from Grayson to her, then flashed her meaningful look. She rolled her eyes.

He merely wrapped an arm around her waist and pulled her closer. Petros had seemed disappointed when she told him she was religious about getting her birth control shot every three months. Since then, he'd been not-so-discretely trying to figure out when her next doctor's appointment was. Kate had a feeling he was going to find some way to convince her to forgo it this next cycle.

"I know what you're thinking. Not gonna happen, buddy," she whispered to him.

"What?" he asked in an innocent tone. "I didn't say anything."

"Ha." She motioned to her stomach, "Nothing's 'ripening' around here anytime soon and don't you be thinking otherwise."

"A man could dream," he said.

"Grayson!" Georgina, Grayson's mother, called as she and her new husband, Luke Lennox, approached them. "Don't just run like that, okay sweetie? Your papa and I were worried."

"Aww, I was just going to Auntie Kate!" he said. "I wanted to say hello."

Kate ruffled the boy's hair. "No harm, no foul." They were surrounded by an entire town of shifters after all. Surely, Grayson was safe.

"You need to stay with us, Grayson," Luke said, his golden eyes darting over to Petros. Jason and Christina had alerted the family about Milos, so of course he would be concerned about his young stepson. "Promise me you won't run away like that again, okay?"

"I promise," he said, then turned to his mother. "Mommy, mommy, Auntie Kate's going to start a garden!"

"A what?" Georgina asked, sending Kate a confused look.

"Auntie Kate she and Uncle Petros were gonna have some ripe fruits!" Grayson exclaimed. "Are you gonna have apples? Or oranges?"

Kate slapped a hand on her forehead. "Uh, something like that."

Georgina looked at Kate, then Petros, and it was like a lightbulb lit up in her head. "Grayson, sweetie! How about some funnel cake?"

"Really? I can have one now?" he asked, his mouth turning up into a big grin.

Luke bent down, picked him up, and put him on his shoulders. "You can have as much as you want."

"Say bye to Auntie Kate and Uncle Petros," Georgina said.

"Bye, Auntie Kate! Bye, Uncle Petros!" He waved at them as Luke and Georgina walked away.

Kate glared at Petros, who looked like he was trying his best not to laugh. "Don't you dare say a word."

Kate never thought about having children of her own. While she liked kids, the whole shebang seemed like a big bother. But with Petros … it sounded thrilling and exciting but scary at the same time. Was she even mom material? When she looked up at his handsome and hopeful face, her mind and her heart were screaming yes. Ugh. She didn't want to think about it now.

"Is it time yet?" she asked, hoping to put the subject of babies aside.

"No," he answered. "We just got here. We should at least get something to eat and then maybe do some shopping?"

She held onto his hand. "All right. Whatever the plan is, we'll stick with it."

And so they played the sweet and affectionate couple as they walked around, though that part wasn't hard. Petros seemed extra attentive to her tonight, never letting her hand go and whispering in her ear or nuzzling her neck. If Milos was watching them, it would seem like their guard was down.

But the reality was quite different. Petros not only had a communication piece in his ear, but he was also wearing a GPS tracking device, just in case Milos tried to take him somewhere far away. There were also several agents surrounding the area, some on the rooftops, plus the Blackstone P.D. was well aware of what was happening. They had embedded some plain-clothes officers in the crowd just in case.

As they walked out of the Main Street Bookshop, Petros stopped in his tracks.

"Is it time?" she asked.

He discretely brushed his finger over his earpiece, then nodded. This was it. The plan was for them to start getting frisky, then pretend to find some dark corner far away from the crowd. They plotted out several possible hotspots around Main Street that might be good for an ambush, and they would move to different ones until Milos attacked.

He turned his body toward her and pulled her flush against him. Leaning down, he planted a soft, slow kiss on her mouth.

Kate moaned and slid her palms up his muscled chest. The kiss was sensual, and heat spread over her body as he continued to caress his mouth with hers. When he pulled away, she was dizzy.

"Wow," she said. "Want to get out of here?"

Petros' lips thinned into a straight line. "Kate-mine," he said as he stared deep into her eyes. His gaze traced over her face as if he were memorizing it. "I hope you can forgive me for what I'm going to do," he said.

"What are you saying? We should get out of here now and stop wasting time."

"I can't let you be in harm's way again," he said.

"Petros, stop this," she hissed. "We have a plan. To trap Milos."

"We do," he said, his face turning grim. "But you won't be part of it."

"I—" Kate gasped when she felt something solid, and surprisingly soft, wrap around her wrist. She turned her head, and her gaze crashed against familiar silvery eyes.

"I'm sorry, Kate," Sybil said. She raised her arm, showing off the fuzzy handcuffs that now linked them.

"What? What's going on?"

"Kate-mine," Petros said, snaking a hand behind her head. "I love you. Now and forever."

Petros pulled her in for a kiss. It felt too final for her tastes, but before she could protest, he was gone, disappearing into the crowd.

"No!" She stamped her feet and tried to walk away, but Sybil stood her ground, refusing to let her go. "You traitor!" she cried.

"I'm not going to let that lunatic near you." Sybil's eyes blazed bright with the power of her dragon.

"I—" She looked back toward the direction Petros had gone. "Please Sybil! Let me go to him. Didn't you hear what he said?" Oh God, Petros loved her. He *loved* her. And she didn't even get a chance to say it back to him. Her wolf yowled in pain. It wanted to be with their mate, to be by his side and protect him.

"Why do you think he asked me to do this?" Sybil said. "Can't you see Kate? If Milos even got anywhere near you, Petros would go ballistic. He can't be distracted!"

"This is absurd! I'm not a distraction; I'm his mate!" She tugged at the handcuffs, but Sybil pulled right back. Her dragon was much stronger than her wolf, but Kate didn't give a shit right now. "You know I can cut this down with a swipe of my claws, right?"

"You know I can singe your hair with a fireball from twenty-feet away, right?"

"I hate you!" Kate spat. "I hate you for doing this to me!"

"You're so dramatic," Sybil said with a roll of her eyes. "Kate, calm down and think about it this way: he doesn't want to have to kill his *best friend*, but he would do it if you were in danger. What do you think would happen to Petros if he did ultimately make that choice? He would choose you, of course, but what would that do this mind and to his wolf if he killed his closest childhood friend?"

Kate opened her mouth but shut it quickly. Sybil was right. She would be a distraction, and Petros would have a better chance of taking Milos alive if he wasn't distracted. And of course Sybil agreed to this. Her best friend would do the same if their positions were reversed. "I really do hate you and love you."

Sybil grinned. "I know you do. Now," she placed her free hand on Kate's shoulder, "you know you don't have to worry about him, right? Christina has a plan in place so they can quietly take Milos down and take him back to a holding cell."

"And what are we supposed to do? Twiddle our thumbs and wait?"

Sybil touched her ear, showing Kate she was wearing an earpiece, too. "Once I've secured you, I'm supposed to bring you back to Blackstone Castle."

Kate pouted. "Can't we stay here, please?"

"No. Petros won't make a move until he knows you're far away."

"Fine then," she said, raising their cuffed hands. "Take me away—" Her eyes widened. "Hey, are these the furry handcuffs I gave you for Valentine's Day?"

Sybil's cheeks went pink. "I had to improvise when he asked me to detain you," she said. "Now, c'mon. We gotta go."

Kate let Sybil lead her away, her heart clenching at the thought of being away from Petros while he faced that monster. But her logical brain told her this was the best possible way to take Milos down without anyone getting hurt, including him. When she saw Petros again, though, she was going to give him a piece of her mind, tell him she loved him, and then possibly lock him in a room and fuck his brains out.

Sybil led her to the parking lot behind the mini-mart. "I'm parked over there," she said, nodding at the familiar silver Prius. "I—" The dragon shifter did not get to finish her sentence as a scream of pain escaped her mouth.

"Sybil!"

It happened so fast. There was a blur right behind Sybil one moment and then the next, she was on the ground, moaning in pain, bringing Kate down with her.

"Don't try anything, bitch." Milos was kneeling beside Sybil, a gun trained on her head.

"You!" she said. Her wolf howled in anger, rearing up to

get ready to battle. But she calmed it, at least for now. "What did you do to her?"

Milos' face twisted in anger, and his good eye glowed. "Just a little bloodsbane. It'll wear off in a few hours," he said, referring to the only substance that could fully knock out a shifter. He pressed the barrel of his gun to Sybil's head. "But this is permanent."

Kate's heart slammed into her rib cage. "Don't hurt her!"

"I won't. Not if you do as I say."

"F-f-fine! What do you want?"

Milos grabbed Sybil's limp arm and raised it. "Free yourself."

Kate raised a hand, her fingers turning into razor-sharp claws. For a second, she considered using it on his face but wasn't sure if she could disable him before he pulled the trigger. She brought her paw down, slicing the handcuffs in half.

"Good," Milos said. He reached over and pulled something from Sybil's neck. It was a syringe. "Fuck! I used all of it on her! Damn dragon shifter! No matter." He turned back to Kate and pointed the gun at her. "Get up!"

Kate got to her feet slowly, trying to think of a way to disable Milos. She had done it before, but they weren't in a vehicle now.

"Put your hands behind you," he ordered.

She did as he said, and he moved behind her. Something clamped around her wrists and forced them together—plastic zip ties. Milos pointed the gun to her head. "You try to break those, I'll pull the trigger."

"You can't possibly think you can get away with this!"

"Did you think I didn't know what Petros and the Alpha's daughter was planning?" he said in an eerily calm voice. "I was one of them. Did they forget? Of course I knew he would try to draw me out. And that he would protect you." He spat. "Poor, pathetic, and unloved Petros. Of course, I did not anticipate the dragon shifter to be here." He glanced down at Sybil, who was now fully unconscious. "I would have brought more bloodsbane had I known."

"So, what's the plan then? Kidnap me again and try to draw out Petros?"

He gave a cruel laugh. "We know how that turned out. No," he said, cocking the gun. "I'm simply going to kill you in front of him and watch his world crumble."

Kate swallowed a gulp. This was it. She would die by the hands of this madman tonight and all without Petros knowing how she truly felt about him.

No fucking way. She was Kate *motherfucking* Caldwell. There had to be a way out of this.

"Let her go!"

Oh no.

Petros came out of the shadows. His face was drawn into a mask of fury. "Milos! Your fight is with me. Let her go. Now."

Milos laughed and pulled Kate by the arm. "Ah, good. You're here," he said. "It'll save me the trouble of having to find you."

"Let her go, and we can settle this one on one," Petros said as he advanced on them.

"Don't come any closer!" Milos yelled and pressed the gun to Kate's temple.

"Milos, please," Petros began, his voice soothing. "I … I did not know you were still alive. We were making our retreat, and I thought we were safe. It was my fault."

"It most definitely was!" Milos said.

"You went overboard, and we thought you were long gone," Petros explained.

Milos grit his teeth. "They fished me out of the water and tossed me into a detention center. After I was 'processed,' I was sent to some kind of medical laboratory for testing."

Kate gasped. She had heard of what The Organization had done to shifters in their labs. A visible shiver ran through her.

"Please, Milos," Petros begged. "It is not too late. You have done nothing wrong yet. We can help. Please, let us take you home. Your mother—"

"Fuck you, Petros!" Milos spat. "Do you think I want to live after what they did to me? For my mother to see what I am now? I'm not going to live past tonight. I don't deserve to live, not after what they did to me and *what they made me do!*" He cocked the gun pointed at Kate. "At least I get to see your face when your mate dies in front of you before I leave this Godforsaken earth."

"No!"

"Say goodbye to—"

Milos's voice was drowned out by the loud sounds of whistles and bangs. Overhead the sky lit up with fireworks, part of the festivities happening at the block party. Milos dropped the gun and howled in anguish.

Kate didn't waste any time. She ducked out of the way and then head-butted Milos right in his abdomen. He toppled and fell back, and Kate rolled away just in time as a large wolf soared over her and landed on top of Milos.

Using her shifter strength, Kate tore through the zip ties around her wrists. She stood up and saw Petros' wolf holding down Milos, snapping its jaws at the man cowering underneath him. *Shit.* The fireworks must have triggered something in Milos, probably something they did to him in those labs since he didn't even try to fight back. When she saw Petros' wolf open its jaws, ready to go for Milos' throat, Kate couldn't stop her scream.

"Petros! No!" She ran to him, pushing her body forward like she'd never done before. "Petros, don't kill him."

The wolf looked up at her, its eyes crazed and glowing with anger. Milos remained prone, his face ashen and frozen in fright. He must have been going through some serious PTSD because he wasn't even fighting. Instead, his head was turned to one side, neck exposed and ready.

"Petros, don't." She sank to her knees next to him. "You'll regret it. You can't kill your best friend." Her fingers sank into his soft fur, and she called on her own wolf to try to soothe their mate. Her wolf whimpered an answer, yowling in pain as they both felt their mate's anguish.

The wolf pressed its snout against her face, and slowly it began to ebb away until Petros was kneeling right next to her.

"Petros," she choked. "Thank God."

A flurry of movement made both of them turn their heads. Christina, Jason, and three agents were running toward them. Jason reached them first and hauled Milos to his feet as the three agents worked to secure him in handcuffs. It wasn't difficult as Milos didn't put up a struggle at all. Despite what he had done, Kate couldn't help the ache she felt in her heart as she looked at his cold, lifeless expression.

"They … must have done … something terrible," Petros rasped.

She wanted to answer, but she didn't know what to say. Instead, she wrapped her arms around Petros and squeezed tight.

"Are you all right?" Christina asked as she approached. "We lost contact with Sybil, and we knew something must have happened."

"Sybil!" She looked over to her fallen friend. Jason was already kneeling beside her, trying to revive his sister. "It's bloodsbane. He gave her a whole syringe full. She'll probably be out for hours, but she'll be fine."

"Thank God," Christina said. "What happened?"

Kate quickly told her the events that had transpired. "The fireworks or the noises somehow made him catatonic. Probably PTSD from all those—" She stopped herself, not wanting Petros to hurt any more than he probably already was.

"It's okay," he said as he held onto Kate to get to his feet. "What they did to him ... unacceptable. And my fault."

"No!" Kate protested. "We all know the people running The Organization are complete bastards! If anyone is to blame, it's them!" She turned to Christina. "It's not too late, right? He wasn't fully feral. You can still save him, right?"

"We can try," Christina said, but the expression on her face was tight.

"That's all we need to know," Kate said. "We will do what we can for him. Get him the best psychologist, treatments, rehab—whatever it takes to get him back."

Christina nodded. "Of course. Now, I have things to take care of." She looked over at Jason, who was carrying Sybil away. "You guys should go home. One of the agents can drive you back."

"Thanks," Kate said. "We'll do that."

Both of them remained silent for the rest of the evening. One of the agents had brought Petros some fresh clothes, and he dressed without saying a word. When they got into the car, he was stony and didn't make a sound. Kate sat next to him, unable to speak. Even when they were alone after they got dropped off at the loft, neither of them tried to talk.

When the front door shut behind her, she finally broke the silence. "Petros, talk to me, please. I—" She stopped when he turned and wrapped his arms around her in a tight embrace.

"I thought I had lost you," he murmured against her neck. "When they told me that Sybil wasn't answering her comm, I knew something was wrong. And when I saw him with the gun to your head—"

"Shh." She ran a hand down his back. "I'm here. It's fine. Nothing happened to me."

"You could have died." His voice broke with grief. "And when my wolf came out of me, it was blinded by hate. I nearly killed him."

"But you didn't."

"You stopped me."

"I made you see reason, but you stopped all by yourself," she said. "What happened to Milos was terrible, but you can't blame yourself for that. You didn't do any of those things to him."

"I know, but I am still partly to blame. I was the leader of the team. I chose to leave him behind."

"You were making what you thought was the right choice at that moment. But I promise we will make it right." She pulled away and looked up into the ocean-colored depths of his eyes. "I meant what I said. Whatever needs to be done, we'll do it."

He raised a dark brow. "We?"

She gave him a weak smile. "Of course. We're a package deal now, you and me." She got on her tip toes and kissed him. When she tried to pull away, he held her in place. Petros deepened the kiss, his tongue pushing against her lips to open them.

She moaned, and his hands moved down under her knees. He bent and lifted her up, wrapping her legs around his waist.

He walked them back to her bedroom, his lips never leaving hers. When her back hit the bed, his kisses became urgent and his fingers fumbled at her clothes. He pulled back when she was finally naked, and his gazed raked over her.

"You are exquisite," he said, his eyes boldly devouring every inch of her.

She looked up at him. "And yours."

A soft growl escaped his lips, and he made quick work of his clothes. He stood in front of her, naked and bared, his cock already hard. Fuck, he was so freaking hot. Kate could stare at his chiseled body all day.

He covered her, spreading her thighs to settle between them. "Kate," he said in an urgent voice as the tip of his cock pressed against her entrance. "Finally mine."

She gasped when he pushed inside her with one stroke. "Petros!" she cried as he began to move within her. "Petros, I love you." She heard him suck in a breath, but he didn't break his rhythm.

Kate closed her eyes as a warm feeling began to settle over her. It was like a ribbon, wrapping around them from head to toe and tightening to pull them together until they melded as one. Happiness, excitement, peace, contentment, and all kinds of emotions were crashing around them like waves on the shore. It scared her at first, as she'd never felt anything like it, but deep inside she knew what it was.

"Yes!" she cried out as he moved faster. Her body tightened like a spring, threatening to break. He didn't relent. Instead he moved harder, hitting all the right spots, until she screamed her pleasure. Petros rode the wave with her, urging her forward and pushing her off the edge until her breath came in small pants. Only when her body shuddered in a second, smaller orgasm did he let go, grunting and moaning his own pleasure as he came, his cock pulsing deep into her and filling her with his cum.

They lay there for a few seconds, and when he tried to pull away, she tightened her legs around him. "No. Stay."

Petros relaxed against her. "You're truly my mate now." He kissed her forehead. "The mating bond. I felt it."

"It feels fucking incredible." Her body, her soul, her very being felt tied to him. Yes, she belonged to him, and she didn't feel trapped at all. He was hers, too. Now and forever.

EPILOGUE

Two weeks later...

Petros walked into The Den, glancing around in search of his mate. While he did not make a habit of being late or being away from her if he could help it, he had a good excuse tonight. Well, two good excuses.

First was Milos. Since they caught him, Petros had been by to visit his friend every day. Even though Milos refused to acknowledge his presence, he did not miss a day in the past two weeks. When they first caught him, they detained him in one of the Blackstone Police Department's jail cells. But when he began to swing between catatonic states and raging madness, keeping him there would not be feasible in the long run, and they knew they had to find another permanent solution.

He had gone to visit Milos again today, this time in his new home. They didn't want to send him back to Lykos for fear that the sea or some of his former teammates might trigger one of his episodes. So Matthew Lennox offered one of their unused properties deep in the Blackstone Mountains, an old abandoned Ranger station. They outfitted it to contain Milos and make it livable while they were trying to figure out what happened to him and how to best help him. The drive back was long, but it was worth it. He would visit Milos as much as he could until he eventually came back to his true self.

And his second excuse? He had something very important to take care of, and he couldn't wait to see Kate's face when she saw what it was.

Speaking of which, he had to find his mate. He was thirty minutes late but had sent her a message about the delay, so surely she would not have left without him.

"The nerve of that dickweed!"

Petros followed the sound of Kate's voice and found his mate standing around a table with her usual band of female friends. Sybil, Amelia, and Dutchy listened intently as Kate relayed her story.

"Apologies for the delay," he said as he came up behind her.

Kate's eyes lit up. "Hey, babe!" She kissed him on the cheek. "How's everything?" A look of concern flashed across her face. "How is he?"

"The same."

She slipped an arm around his waist. "Don't worry. He'll get better. I know it."

The look of absolute faith on his mate's face made the heaviness in his chest disappear. Indeed, whenever he found himself feeling bothered or burdened, her mere presence soothed him. He knew Milos' recovery would be a long one, but knowing Kate would be by his side would make the process much easier on him and his wolf. He leaned down and pressed his lips to hers, enjoying the soothing balm of her kiss.

He didn't want it to end, but when someone cleared their throat, he pulled away and turned to the other women. The three girls were giving them knowing but joyful looks.

"Apologies for interrupting ladies," he said. "Please continue."

"Kate was just telling us about how she lost that eBay auction," Amelia Walker said.

Now that the bear shifter was in the process of moving back to Blackstone, Petros had seen more of his mate's friend, and Kate's joy was almost palpable. He found he liked the even-tempered and practical Amelia a lot, and she was a good balance to the trio she, Sybil, and Kate made.

"I did *not* lose! That twaffletwat seller! I swear I could wring his neck!" Kate raised a fist. "I had the highest bid, but he withdrew the auction last night. I emailed him for an explanation, and all he said was he got a better offer for the Chevelle."

"Kate's been tearing up a storm," Dutchy said, taking a sip of her wine. "Says she's going to hack the guy's email to find out who the buyer was."

"I wouldn't want to get on Kate's bad side," Sybil said.

"Revenge is her game," Amelia added with a laugh. "As we know."

"Wait, what happened?" Dutchy asked, catching the look that passed between the three friends. "What did Kate do?"

Sybil's face fell. "It's nothing! I mean, we shouldn't—"

"It's fine," Kate said. "We can talk about Tommy."

Petros' spine went rigid, but when Kate gave him a reassuring squeeze, he relaxed. If his mate was all right talking about her ex-boyfriend, then he could be, too.

"After we finally broke up," Kate said, "he went around spreading rumors about me. That I was easy and cheated on him with a ton of other guys."

Petros couldn't help the growl that escaped his throat at what that bastard did to her. Perhaps he wouldn't be okay with it right now, but he would learn. It was all in the past after all.

"So I did what I had to do." Kate had a smug smile on her face. "I hacked into his computer. And by hacked I mean, I guessed his password was 'poopchute123' for his laptop and just about all his online accounts. I found this video of him on his hard drive." Her mouth curled up into an evil smile. "It was of him doing a cover of this super cheesy love song. It was horrible, not just because of his voice, but because he was *really* into it. He was even dressed up like a '90s boy band member."

"It was a full music video and had all these corny hearts and flower effects," Sybil added.

"It was hilarious," Amelia said, doubling over and clutching her stomach as she laughed. "At one point, I believe he was singing to his favorite stuffed rabbit."

"Mr. Sprinkles!" Sybil remembered with a snap of her fingers.

"And I posted it on all of his social media accounts," Kate said proudly.

"Don't forget the jumbotron at the football field during homecoming," Sybil added.

"And the TV screens all over school," Amelia said. "It took them days to find the source of the feed."

Sybil put her arm around Amelia and nodded. *"And my love is ooooonly for youuuuuu ...."* They crooned in unison before bursting into a fit of giggles.

"Oh yeah!" Kate wiped the tears from her eyes. "Well, after that, his reputation as a bad boy pretty much was torn to shreds. He didn't come back the next year."

"Remind me never to get on your bad side," Petros said. Hopefully, Kate would only be a bit mad at him for what he had done. Which reminded him ... "I hate to pull you away from your friends, but I haven't had my supper," he said. "Perhaps we could head to the diner?"

"Oh, sorry, babe, didn't realize you hadn't eaten yet." She grabbed her purse. "I'll see you guys around." With a final wave, they set off toward the exit.

Petros held the door open and let Kate out first. As he let the door close behind him, he nearly bumped into his mate, who stood frozen in her spot. "Is anything the matter?"

"Hey man, what's up?" Mason Grimes greeted as the storm door shut behind him.

"Mason, nice to see you again," Petros greeted. He truly was grateful for the man who had saved his mate, even if Kate was still furious.

Kate grimaced. "I thought I smelled something rotten in here."

"Look, Kate," Mason said. "I'm not here to cause trouble, okay? I'm in Blackstone to sort a couple of things out."

"Oh yeah? How's your *wife*?"

It was Mason's turn to grimace. "*Ex*-wife," he corrected. "I've been divorced for over a year."

"Well congratu-fucking-lations," Kate spat back. "You guys lasted longer than I thought."

Mason let out a deep sigh. "Some things never change. Well, you seem like a nice guy," he said to Petros, "so maybe I'll see you around town." The polar bear shifter turned and lumbered into the bar, his shoulders hunched over and his hands in his pockets.

Petros looked at his mate with deep concern. "He was married? I thought you said he was Amelia's ex-boyfriend?" Perhaps Mason wasn't the man he thought he was.

"He *wasn't* married when they met," Kate huffed. "Its complicated."

"But his presence still upsets you? Even after he saved your life?"

A sudden anger lit her eyes. "And thus the only reason he's still breathing. What he did—oh crap!" She turned around, facing the door back into The Den. "Amelia! Oh shit. She's in there, and she's gonna see him! I have to go—"

Petros gently wrapped a hand around her arm. "Kate-mine," he said in a soothing voice. "Amelia is a grown woman and a mature and level-headed person. She doesn't need you to fight her battles for her." When Kate frowned at him, he kissed the wrinkle between her brows. "But I know you would do it because she is your friend. Still, when it comes to matters of the heart, perhaps it's best to leave her be. It's the one thing she must figure out herself."

Kate looked like she wanted to protest, but then sighed in defeat. "You're right," she said. "But Amelia's going to be furious at me when she finds I out I knew about him moving here and didn't tell her."

"Maybe for a while," he said. "But she will forgive you. Now," he gave her another kiss, "can we go?" He hoped the surprise he had been planning would make her forget about her worries.

Kate nodded. "All right."

He led her out into the parking lot, down to the very last row. Anticipation pumped through his veins, not just because of the surprise he had planned, but the very important thing that would come after.

"Where's your pickup truck?" she said, looking around.

"I didn't drive it today. I had to go pick something up."

"Is that so?" she asked. "What?"

He stopped and then cocked his head to the left. "That."

"I don't—What. The. *Fuck*." Kate's jaw dropped, and her eyes went wide. "Petros! What is this?"

The electric blue Chevelle was parked in the last spot, looking shiny and new. He had paid the seller extra to have it delivered today, and then brought it to J.D.'s garage for a once-over, as well as a quick wax and shine. The mechanic was only happy to drive it to The Den after finding out who it was for.

She slapped him on the shoulder. "It was you! *You* were the buyer!"

He nodded. "Will you forgive me, Kate-mine? For being sneaky and not telling you?"

"But why?" she asked, her eyes still glossing over the car, her expression full of disbelief.

"Because it was a surprise," he said. His heart began to pound in his chest. "And knowing your aversion to gifts, I thought this would be a better way to ask you to marry me than with a ring."

"You—what?"

"Kate-mine," he got down on one knee, "will you marry me?"

"I—wait. You got me an engagement *car*?"

"Of course," he said. "I asked your father for his blessing the other day and that gave me the idea."

"You talked to my dad? I haven't even introduced you guys yet."

Petros didn't want to wait any longer than he had to, so he asked Jason Lennox to make the introduction over video call. Clark and Martha Caldwell were both stunned but ultimately happy at the news.

"That's the proper way, is it not?" he asked. "But will you kindly answer my question? Before I start growing fungus down here?"

Kate chuckled. "And they said you didn't have a funny bone in your body." She leaned down and kissed him. "And yes, I will marry you."

He got up and took her into his arms. Warmth, comforting and serene, flowed through him as his mate relaxed against his body. The bond was growing stronger every day, a fact that pleased him.

"Hmm," she sighed. "You're happy."

"Very much so."

"I can feel it," she said. "Since we bonded, it's like I can feel everything you feel. And even when you're not around, it's like you're here," she said, placing a hand over her heart. She looked up at him. "Does it feel the same for you?"

"Yes," he said with a nod. "And something else."

"What?"

He smiled down at her. "It feels like home."

The story continues in

The Blackstone She-Bear
Available on Amazon

Want to read a (**hot, sexy and explicit**) extended scene from this book?

Sign up for my newsletter here:
http://aliciamontgomeryauthor.com/mailing-list/

You'll get access to ALL the bonus materials from all my books and my **FREE** novella **The Last Blackstone Dragon.**

ABOUT THE AUTHOR

Alicia Montgomery has always dreamed of becoming a romance novel writer. She started writing down her stories in now long-forgotten diaries and notebooks, never thinking that her dream would come true. After taking the well-worn path to a stable career, she is now plunging into the world of self-publishing.

facebook.com/aliciamontgomeryauthor
twitter.com/amontromance
bookbub.com/authors/alicia-montgomery

Printed in Dunstable, United Kingdom